On WINGS of MAGIC

on WINGS of MAGIC

Kay Hooper

Loveswept

Doubleday

New York · London · Toronto · Sydney · Auckland

LOVESWEPT®

PUBLISHED BY DOUBLEDAY

a division of Bantam Doubleday Dell Publishing Group, Inc.
1540 Broadway, New York, New York 10036

DOUBLEDAY, LOVESWEPT, and the portrayal of the wave device
are trademarks of Doubleday, a division of
Bantam Doubleday Dell Publishing Group, Inc.

Published by arrangement with the author.

Library of Congress Catologing-in-Publication Data

Hooper, Kay
On wings of magic / Kay Hooper.
p.   cm.
"Loveswept."
1. Bahamas—Fiction.   I. Title.
PS3558.O587O5   1993
813'.54—dc20   93-6661   CIP

ISBN 0-385-47152-1

Design by Diane Stevenson / Snap·Haus Graphics

All Rights Reserved

Printed in the United States of America

November 1993

1   3   5   7   9   10   8   6   4   2

On Wings of Magic

C h a p t e r

1

awke Madison listened absently to his manager enthusiastically reading the names of important guests for the summer, his mind only half on the conversation. His hooded gaze was wandering around the sumptuously appointed lobby, flickering with satisfaction at the restful yet luxurious atmosphere which he had painstakingly created.

Skimming over the marble floor, dotted here and there with lush greenery and comfortable chairs and divans, his gray eyes fell at last on the wide glass doors and the doorman who was standing stiffly outside them. He watched Max step forward to greet someone—apparently another guest—and smiled inwardly as he mentally went through the routine greeting. Max would be coolly polite, stiffly British, easily upholding the high-class air of the establishment.

Max was a good doorman, Hawke thought to himself. And a first-rate bouncer, although his haughty, intimidating manner rarely made physical force necessary. Yes, Max was a good employee. Max was . . . smiling. Smiling? *Max?*

Curiously, Hawke waited to see who would come through the doors. Max, Hawke was sure, wouldn't smile at the queen of England. But he was smiling now. And it was a peculiar smile at that. Shy, bemused, like a ray of sunshine emerging. Impatiently waving his manager to silence, he stared at the door.

First through the door was a cabdriver, huffing under the weight of a ton of luggage that bore labels from every country in the world Hawke had heard of, and a few he hadn't. The cabdriver's face was wearing the same bemused smile as Max's. Hawke had never, in his five years as the owner of this hotel, seen a cabdriver even *offer* to carry luggage.

Next through the door was Max, leaving his post and apparently not even aware of it. His graying head was bent attentively to catch the bubbling conversation of the vision who had one small, delicate hand resting confidingly on his arm.

Everything about her was an odd combination of sweet helplessness and exotic mystery. Her silver-blond hair was styled in a smooth pageboy, framing a heart-shaped face as delicate and lovely as that of a porcelain doll. Huge, innocent blue-green eyes dominated the face, and gave her the unguarded look of a newborn kitten. A lime-green silk dress hugged a figure that had heads turning all across the large lobby; it was slit on one side almost to her hip, exposing a seductive length of golden thigh with every step.

And there was a stole draped around her neck—a *live* stole. Hawke's first thought was that the yellow-and-black-spotted creature was a baby leopard, but then the word *ocelot* popped into his mind. It was about the size of a very large housecat, with yellow eyes blinking detached interest at the commotion all around it.

Feeling anything but detached, Hawke watched bemusedly as his new guest walked gracefully across the lobby on the arm of an obviously ensnared Max, and just barely caught a fragment of her soft conversation.

". . . and it was such a *crush* at the airport! Is it always like that, Max?" she bubbled sweetly, her voice filled with music. "I've never been to the Bahamas before. . . ."

Chaos reigned all around her. Two bellboys were arguing fiercely with the cabdriver, who was loath to give up the luggage. One guest walked into a potted palm in an effort to get a better view of the enchantress, while another ran smack into the argument going on over the luggage . . . and promptly became the target of blue-tinted invective from the cabdriver. Both the desk clerk and Hawke's manager stood openmouthed with astonishment. Or awe.

And through it all walked the new guest, with an indifference that was apparently the product of innocence rather than arrogance.

She paused to speak sweetly to the cabdriver and, though Hawke didn't hear what she said, it was apparent that the big, beefy man would willingly have killed for her. He abandoned the luggage finally, backing out the door with his hat literally in his hand.

Reaching the desk at last, she went through the formality of registering, still talking a mile a minute to both the desk clerk and Max—both of whom were patently captivated. A little boy came barreling around from in back of the desk just then, running into the new guest with a force that staggered her. Instead of being annoyed, she knelt down to be on eye level with the boy, speaking to him and smiling gently.

A beautiful, ultrafeminine woman, Hawke was thinking delightedly, who obviously loved kids. God—he had believed that type of woman to be an extinct species! Heaven knew it was a change from the coolly sophisticated, ambitious women he was accustomed to, and a far cry from those who were so wrapped up in the women's lib movement that they fairly bit a man's head off for opening a door for them!

He watched as she patted the boy's cheek and rose, seeing the adoring look on the child's face and not surprised by it. He was still watching moments later as she was escorted to the elevator. Then, leaving his silent manager without a word, he walked over to the desk and checked the register. Kendall James. *Miss* Kendall James. He glanced thoughtfully toward the elevator, a definite gleam in his gray eyes.

On Wings of Magic

❦ ❦

Kendall closed the door at last as the bellboy left and leaned against it with a weary sigh. God, but she was tired! The flight from Paris hadn't been too bad, but the week before had been hectic. She'd kept herself too busy to do more than tumble into bed at night and sleep dreamlessly—exactly as she'd wanted to do. It was a sort of therapy for her.

Like the performance downstairs. After twenty-five years, she had the routine down pat. It was a rare talent, her father had once humorously remarked, a peculiar ability to be exactly what people—particularly men—expected her to be. So . . . if an uncertain smile or a helpless look got her the best tables in restaurants or a seat on a supposedly booked-solid flight to wherever . . . terrific.

Kendall was a realist. She looked like the proverbial dumb blonde and she knew it. She didn't resent that fact, nor did she go through life aggressively demanding that people realize she was no such thing. She used it. Men bent over backward to do things for her: They certainly enjoyed it, and she didn't have to carry her own luggage. A fine arrangement all around.

Absently setting her ocelot on the plushly carpeted floor, she watched the cat begin to explore, her mind still on her masquerade downstairs. Not that it was really a masquerade. It was more a part of herself that she allowed to take control for a time. She *was* a very feminine woman. Men instinctively wanted

to watch over her, to protect her, thinking her touchingly innocent. That was fine with Kendall. She had nothing to prove to
anyone; she felt neither inferior nor superior to any man—or to
anyone, for that matter.

Besides . . . there was a certain devilish enjoyment in
watching men fall over potted palms.

Kendall smiled as she remembered the poor man who had
caused that hilarious display in the lobby, then wondered
vaguely about the dark-looking man. He'd watched her, she
remembered, the entire time she'd been in the lobby. There
had been several men around, but he stood out in her mind for
several reasons. First because of his clothing. He'd been wearing a black suit—the color unusual for the tropics, and the
formality unusual for afternoon attire even in this classy hotel.

He was a hard-looking man, she'd noted, a man who
looked as though he'd seen a few of life's more than usually
unpleasant truths. The strength beneath his well-cut clothing
had been apparent, and the harshly drawn features attractive in
an oddly primitive, compelling way. It would not be possible,
she thought, to ignore such a man. He would be either loved or
hated—and possibly both at the same time.

Frowning, Kendall pushed the absurd thoughts away. She
was here to rest, to allow her nerves to unwind after those
harrowing months in South America. Her father would join her
in a few weeks, and they'd be off again. Probably to the Middle

East, although her father hadn't been sure about that. In any case, she had a few weeks to laze around in paradise.

So. She'd work on her tan, write letters to friends, and act like a scatterbrained tourist. Heaven knew, she didn't need another emotional upheaval in her life. When one had a great deal in common with a rolling stone, it hurt too much to form attachments. And Kendall hated saying good-bye.

The sound of the bathroom faucets being turned on full force distracted her suddenly, and Kendall flung her purse on the huge bed and headed hastily for the bathroom. "Gypsy! Drat you, cat—turn that water off! I've *told* you before . . ."

Two hours later Kendall had completed her unpacking and cleaned up the mess her pet had made in the beautiful green-tiled bathroom. Leaving her cat to sun herself while leashed on the balcony—where, Kendall hoped, she wouldn't decide to test her flying ability—Kendall changed into one of her more modest bathing suits and an ankle-length terry cover-up, grabbed her beachbag, and headed for the inviting pool behind the hotel.

Emerging from the elevator in the lobby and pausing to get her bearings, she overheard a snatch of conversation between the desk clerk and one of the bellboys, and felt her interest pique.

"Did you see the gleam in his eye?" the young woman was

laughingly asking. "Mark my words—the hawk's going hunting!"

The blond bellboy responded mournfully. "Yeah—but this time he's going after a hummingbird! The poor little thing won't stand a chance. Think we should warn her?"

"And miss what'll probably be the best entertainment of the summer? No way!"

The elevator doors opened behind her, and Kendall hastily slung the beachbag over her shoulder and crossed the lobby. She smiled sunnily at the pair by the desk, waved, and immediately noted their twin expressions of consternation. *Oh, no!* she thought with rueful amusement. *That means I'm the intended prey!* A hummingbird, huh? Well, she'd probably been called worse. Translated: a pretty, helpless, fluttery creature.

And, quite suddenly, her father's parting words to her made far more sense than they had at the time. "Beware of the hawk!" he'd told her with a laugh as she'd boarded the plane in South America. But who was the hawk? And how did her father know him—or know of him?

Kendall had a sudden uneasy feeling that her father had been in one of his infrequent alarmingly scheming moods when he'd chosen this resort for her. And the last time *that* had happened, she'd found herself very nearly engaged. It had taken some fancy footwork to get herself out of the mess, and she'd retaliated by doing some unsubtle matchmaking of her own. Alarmed, the elder James had stopped pushing.

It wasn't that he wanted to get rid of her and figured that a husband was the best way, Kendall mused wryly as she stepped out into the bright sunlight and headed for an unoccupied lounge by the pool. It was simply her father's belief—unequivocally stated more than once—that following him, a mining engineer, into some of the more godforsaken areas of the world was not the life he wanted for his daughter. She didn't really blame him for that; she understood completely. But she enjoyed travel and was perfectly capable of taking care of herself—even her father admitted that.

The past fifteen years *had* complicated her love life, though. And not just because she was rarely in one place long enough to form more than a surface relationship. Through wry experience, Kendall knew that her ability to take care of herself had jarred more than one male ego. It probably had a great deal to do with the fact that she looked so feminine and so ridiculously helpless, she thought. And her near-constant charade hadn't helped.

Pushing the thoughts away, Kendall dropped her bag on the lounge she had selected, untied her cover-up, and allowed it to drop to the multicolored tiles surrounding the tremendous pool. She stepped out of her thongs and strolled to the edge of the pool, never noticing that one rather paunchy guest choked on his drink and another grossly offended his female companion by staring at Kendall for a full minute.

The black bikini was the most modest one in Kendall's

wardrobe, but only the liberal-minded would have believed that. The best thing that could have been said for it was that it probably wouldn't get her arrested. It was a string bikini, with tiny black triangles covering what absolutely had to be covered and not a fraction of an inch more. And since her petite figure was surprisingly voluptuous, the effect was distinctly eye-catching.

Unconcerned with the attention she had attracted, Kendall cautiously stuck one toe in the water, then took a deep breath and dived cleanly off the side. Without pausing, she swam the length of the pool twice, displaying the smooth coordination of a skilled swimmer. Her earlier weariness dissipated by the brisk exercise, she headed for the shallow end of the pool feeling refreshed and alert.

A male hand was extended to help her up the steps, and Kendall took it automatically, her widening eyes fixed in utter fascination on the colorful bird drawn with a skillful hand on the tanned forearm. No doubt about it—it was a hawk.

"Oh," she murmured, still staring at the tattoo. "Then *that's* the hawk!"

"No—I am," returned the amused and startlingly deep masculine voice that obviously owned the tattoo.

"Hawk like the bird?" she inquired innocently, raising her gaze to meet a pair of striking light-gray eyes, and thinking insanely, *Oh, no! Anybody but him!*

The dark man from the lobby laughed and assisted her up

the steps. "Hawk with an *e*. I'm Hawke Madison, Miss James. I own the hotel."

"Kendall—please," she murmured, holding on to her charade with an effort and wondering ruefully if the next few weeks were going to be as restful as she had supposed. Without bothering to dry off, she moved her beachbag and sank down on the lounge, feeling more than a little unnerved and wondering why.

"Only if you'll call me Hawke." He sank down on the lounge beside her own, smiling with devastating effect.

Kendall's veiled gaze swept his muscular length, noting that he had changed out of the suit and into a pair of casual slacks and a knit sport shirt. Trying to ignore the rapid-fire pace of her heart, she said sweetly, "That shouldn't be hard to remember," and nodded at the small but colorful tattoo.

One large hand brushed over the hawk as he laughed. "I'm afraid I can't be held responsible for this, Kendall. A couple of army buddies decided years ago that I should wear my name on my arm, so to speak, and they took care of it."

"Didn't it hurt?" she asked curiously.

"To be perfectly truthful, I can't remember," he confessed with an absurdly shamefaced expression.

She considered his answer for a moment and bit the inside of her lip to keep from laughing. "You were drunk?"

"They never would have gotten me into the tattoo parlor otherwise," he explained gravely.

As Hawke talked more about his past, Kendall's first instinct was to abandon her charade and get to know this fascinating man, but she swiftly discarded the notion. She did *not* want a summer fling, and after overhearing the desk clerk and bellboy in the lobby, she was fairly certain that was all Hawke Madison had in mind. And if she were, by chance, wrong about what he wanted from her, the situation could become dangerous for her peace of mind.

Smiling at him sunnily, she began to chatter, knowing from experience that few things put a man off quicker than an extremely talkative woman. She talked a great deal without saying a thing, sprinkling the one-sided conversation with questions she barely gave Hawke time to answer and jumping from topic to topic bewilderingly.

Half an hour later Hawke was called from the poolside to answer a phone call. Rummaging in her bag for her sunglasses, Kendall shoved them onto her nose and decided a bit grimly that she was definitely in trouble. Hawke Madison had the patience of Job. He'd answered each breathless question with amused indulgence, and seemed fascinated by her empty chatter. Now what?

Kendall wasn't vain by any means. She knew that men found her to be attractive and she knew that her figure was good. But she'd always admired darkly exotic beauty, and her own reflection in a mirror always reminded her of a startled kitten. Startled kittens were cute, but they weren't beautiful.

A lot of men, apparently, liked cute women. Kendall had met some ranging from polished charmers to blunt, few-worded engineers. There had even been an Arabian sheikh who had very nearly swept her off her feet in an unguarded moment. But she had generally managed to emerge scatheless from the romantic interludes.

She had an awful feeling, though, that Hawke wasn't going to fit into any of her neat little categories. And that meant that past experience wasn't going to do her a damn bit of good when it came to dealing with him.

It made her distinctly uneasy to be playing a game in which she hadn't the foggiest idea of the rules. And something told her that Hawke was an excellent gamesman.

So . . . her safest bet would be to stick with her protective coloration. Play dumb—at least until she figured out the rules of this game. And the stakes . . .

Hawke returned to her side on the heels of this decision, and she managed to greet him with an unclouded smile. Innocently, she asked, "Should you be taking the time to talk to me like this? I mean—you're obviously busy, and—"

"I'll make the time to talk to you, honey," he replied easily, reclaiming his lounge.

Kendall was tempted to snap that a forty-five-minute acquaintance hardly gave him the right to call her honey, but bit back the words with an inward sigh. It wouldn't be in character, after all, for her to object. Dammit.

"Besides," he was going on calmly, "I don't have much time where you're concerned, do I? Relationships generally take months to develop, but you're planning to be here for only a few weeks. I have to move fast if I plan to get anywhere."

Kendall glared through the shielding sunglasses and wondered if he openly stalked—or was it hunted?—every woman he set his sights on, or if this was simply his tactic for dumb blondes. Either way, she didn't like it. Abruptly deciding not to be as dumb as all that, she raised one eyebrow above the rim of her glasses and murmured blandly, "Where have I heard that line before?"

"All over the world, I'd imagine," he responded dryly, a definite gleam in his eye. "Judging by your suitcases, you've been pretty nearly everywhere, and men are the same no matter where you go."

She pulled the sunglasses down her nose and peered over the top of them at him. Ignoring the rueful statement on his own sex, she said with all the sweet innocence she could muster, "I've never approved of summer romances, Hawke. They tend to fizzle out as soon as the weather starts to cool."

"But we're in the subtropics." He smiled slowly. "It's hot all year round."

Kendall hastily pushed the glasses back up her nose, torn between irritation and amusement and unsure which emotion was showing in her eyes. Oh, she would have to watch herself with this man! She sensed that he was utterly determined . . .

and determined men were dangerous. *Dumb,* she reminded herself sternly. *Play dumb!* "I came here to rest, Hawke," she told him earnestly.

"Rest from what?" He was smiling, but his eyes were intent.

Caught off guard because he had taken her words literally, Kendall automatically told him the truth. "There was some trouble in South America."

"South America? I understood you flew into Nassau from Paris."

Which would teach her not to be so expansive with bellhops and taxi drivers, Kendall thought ruefully. "Oh, I did. But I spent only a week in Paris; before that I was in South America." She had no intention of telling him why she had given in to her father's demand that she leave South America after the revolution broke out.

"What was in South America? Or is that an indelicate question?"

Kendall couldn't see any reason why she shouldn't tell him that—she couldn't see any reason why she *should* either. "My father," she heard herself replying. "He's a mining engineer."

"I see." He leaned forward to brush a hovering insect away from her upper thigh, and Kendall felt an unfamiliar shiver radiating outward from the base of her spine. "What kind of trouble, Kendall?"

"A revolution." The answer came without her volition,

and sounded stilted even to her own ears. She stared into the curiously intense gray eyes, and felt suddenly that she had stepped into deep water and something—someone—was trying to pull her under.

It was his eyes, she realized abruptly. This man possessed more power in his eyes than most men could boast of in their entire bodies. Once, some years before, a friend of her father's had gotten into a long, involved discussion with Kendall about what he called a "leadership quality" in men. There were some men, he had insisted, who were born to lead. They were "alpha" males, dominant, powerful. Striding through life with absolute self-knowledge and certainty.

Kendall hadn't really been able to grasp the concept— probably because she hadn't been able to relate it to anyone she knew. But the man had insisted that *she* was a member of that curious group of dominant personalities. He'd told her that it was her "alpha" instincts that allowed her to play the feather-headed innocent with such ease and to such good effect. She was so certain of herself, he'd said, that she felt no need to prove anything to anyone. And he'd expressed a wistful desire to be a fly on the wall when she finally bumped into an "alpha" male.

He hadn't warned her what to expect in the unlikely possibility that such an event would occur. But she distinctly remembered him muttering something about the clash of the Titans.

Now she knew what he meant.

Hawke Madison was an "alpha" male. For all his charm and amiable conversation, for all his polished, sophisticated manner—probably garnered in his trade as a hotelier—his was a pose just as deft, and just as unreal, as her own.

Kendall couldn't help but wonder which of them would abandon the charade first.

She tore her eyes from his with a silent gasp and thanked heaven for the sunglasses. Trying desperately to get the conversation back to unimportant things, she said lightly, "I didn't expect this island to be so large. How large is it, by the way? When I flew over from Nassau in that little plane, I just closed my eyes."

Hawke was still regarding her with that smile that was doing peculiar things to her nervous system. "It's big," he murmured, giving Kendall the unsettling impression that his mind was on something else. "There's a decent-size village a couple of miles away that caters to tourists, half a dozen churches, a nice harbor with sailboats for rent. There's even another hotel on the other side of the island."

"Competition?" she asked innocently.

"Friendly competition." He laughed. "They cater more to families. With the casino here, we attract a slightly more sophisticated crowd."

Kendall looked toward the shallow end of the pool, where

several dark-skinned children were playing noisily, and then looked back at Hawke with a questioning lift of her brows.

"Kids from the village," he explained with a slight shrug. "I let them use the pool in the afternoons." He gestured toward one of the little boys. "Robbie—the one who ran into you in the lobby."

Looking back at the children, Kendall noted silently that Robbie hadn't, apparently, been scolded or forbidden the pool for nearly knocking down a guest. A little thing, perhaps, but it told Kendall a great deal. Hawke liked kids. She was vaguely irritated with herself for finding something they had in common.

"Excuse me, Hawke." A fair-haired man with an easy smile was gazing down at them both apologetically. "You confirmed some of these reservations personally, and I need to know—"

"Of course, Rick," Hawke interrupted calmly, reaching for the sheaf of papers in the other man's hand. "Kendall, this is my manager, Rick Evans. Rick—Kendall James," he said absently as his eyes scanned the papers.

Kendall smiled at the manager. "Mr. Evans. It's nice to meet you."

"Miss James." His cheerful brown eyes swept her bikini-clad figure with pure masculine appreciation, even as they laughed in familiarity. "My pleasure—believe me!"

Wishing vaguely that Rick's boss could be as uncomplicated as he was, Kendall listened as they began going over the reservations list. A few minutes later she absently pushed her sunglasses up to rest on top of her head, her gaze fixed on the children in the pool as she tuned out the conversation going on beside her. She watched the kids splashing happily and, unbidden, her mind wondered how some children could have so much and others so little. Did any of these happy, healthy kids know what it meant to barely have enough water to drink and none to wash in? Surrounded by what most people would call paradise, did they know that there were children in the world who lived on a heartbeat, hungry and cold and scared in war-torn lands?

A tiny face, pinched from too many years of an empty belly, swam before her inner eye. A face with a smile like sunshine and brown eyes sweet enough to melt a stone statue, eyes innocent and loving in spite of the cruelties they had seen . . .

Kendall winced and gently pushed the face and the memory back into the dark corner of her mind once again. She wasn't ready to face that. Not yet.

"What's wrong, honey?"

Startled, she surfaced from an inescapable past into an equally inescapable present. The manager had gone; she and Hawke were alone. And his gray eyes were filled with concern.

"N-nothing." She corrected the stammer immediately, astonished that her lifelong control was slipping rapidly, inexplicably from her grasp. "What could be wrong?"

"I don't know." His deep voice was serious. "You looked so sad. And there was something . . . old in your eyes."

"Old?" Kendall laughed lightly, more shaken than she wanted to admit—even to herself. Deliberately misunderstanding him, she went on sweetly. "I'm only twenty-five, Hawke—my eyes can't possibly be any older than that."

For a moment she thought that he was going to press her for a reasonable answer to his question. But then heavy lids dropped to veil his strange eyes. "My mistake," he murmured with an almost imperceptible hint of dryness in his tone. "It must have been sunlight glinting off the water. Or something."

A wise little voice inside Kendall warned that she could land herself in a hell of a lot of trouble by playing too dumb with this man. For the first time in many years, Kendall ignored the voice. Her motivation for the decision wasn't very rational, and the little voice sneered at her.

She was afraid of Hawke Madison. Not physically. She was afraid because her body was sending strange signals to her brain, because his eyes were making wordless promises. She was afraid because he saw too much and sensed even more, because he was damnably attractive. Because he was an "alpha" male, and she didn't know how to cope with him. She was afraid because the desire she saw in his eyes was echoed by nameless yearnings in herself, and that had never—ever—happened before.

And she clung to her charade because it possessed the comforting familiarity of a well-worn shoe.

"Have you always traveled with your father?" he asked casually, breaking into her thoughts.

They were back to square one. Dammit. "Ever since I was ten," she answered sunnily.

"And your mother?"

Kendall reached up to pull her sunglasses back into place. "She died when I was five." Before he could make any response, she went on chattily. "What about you, Hawke? You're obviously American—how did you wind up here in paradise?"

He sat back in his lounge and shrugged slightly, the gray eyes still hooded. "I saw quite a bit of the world when I was in the army. When I got out, it seemed natural to go into the hotel business; my family owns a string of hotels in the States. I came here, liked the area, and bought this hotel. That was five years ago."

With a certain deliberation he went on. "I'm thirty-four, unmarried, reasonably intelligent. My favorite color is green, I love Italian food and mood music, children and animals. I don't bite my nails, grind my teeth, or snore."

Trying not to laugh, she said, "Well . . . that takes care of the vital statistics."

"I've also recently discovered a weakness for pint-size blondes."

"How recently?" she demanded suspiciously, forgetting the role she was supposed to be playing.

"A few hours ago. At precisely one-fifteen, as a matter of fact." His deep voice was amused, but not in the least teasing.

Kendall didn't have to think back to remember where she had been at one-fifteen. She'd been walking through the door of this hotel. "Weaknesses like that could become dangerous," she retorted, reaching to brush a strand of drying blond hair away from her face.

"Only if a man doesn't know what he's getting into. I do."

Annoyed by the certainty in his voice, and not entirely sure that they weren't talking at cross-purposes, Kendall hastily reverted to the scatterbrained tourist. "I'll bet you've said exactly the same thing to hundreds of other women since you started running this hotel!" she exclaimed with a giggle.

"Nope. Just you."

"Didn't that line work with the others?"

"I didn't try it." He leaned forward suddenly, heavy lids lifting to reveal gray eyes glittering with a curious laughing intensity. "Because it isn't a line, Kendall. Consider yourself warned—I'm going to do my damnedest to sweep you right off your feet."

She stared at him blankly for a moment. Right offhand the only thing she could have said about his tactics was that they were certainly original. Hadn't he just announced his intention of seducing her? "I—consider myself warned," she managed to say at last, only dimly noticing the breathlessness of her voice.

Having made his point, Hawke—oddly enough—didn't press. He started talking casually about the island, promising cheerfully to take her sailing in a few days. Or shopping or sight-seeing—whatever she liked. The moment of intensity had passed.

Kendall was grateful for the opportunity to relax a bit—although her instincts warned against relaxing too much around this man. She responded to him lightly, talking a great deal without saying very much. Absently, she noticed the children being herded away from the pool by a tanned young man —apparently a lifeguard—and didn't think much about it when one of them slipped away from the group.

The poolside guests had all headed back inside sometime later, and Kendall was beginning to think about going in herself. As she chattered brightly, her eyes wandered around the now-deserted pool and back to Hawke's face. And then something clicked in her mind, and she knew that the dark shape near the pool's bottom didn't belong there. In a single motion she ripped the sunglasses off and rose to her feet, her chatter shutting off as though a switch had been thrown. Two swift steps took her to the edge of the pool, and she dived cleanly, intent only on reaching the child in time.

C h a p t e r

I

t was Robbie, the little boy who had run into her in the lobby, and Kendall's heart clenched in fear even as she caught him and propelled them both to the surface. She was barely aware of strong hands reaching for the boy as they reached the edge of the pool, allowing Hawke to pull him from the water as she herself hastily climbed up onto the tiles. He barely had time to lay the still child gently on the tiles before Kendall was there, immediately beginning the resuscitation techniques she'd been taught long ago.

Unaware that a shocked, silent crowd had gathered, Kendall worked grimly. Silently, fiercely, she vowed that she would not allow another child to die if she could help it. "Breathe," she whispered, utterly determined. *"Breathe,* dammit!"

At last the boy coughed weakly and retched, and Kendall rolled him onto his side, thumping him on the back to expel the last of the water. She was too relieved to notice the buzz of admiring conversation from the surrounding group, feeling a tremor possess her now, in the aftermath of unbearable tension. She held the scared, sobbing child to her breast, murmuring soothingly until he was relatively calm.

"I'll take him, Miss James." It was Hawke's manager, Rick, speaking in a gruff voice as he stepped forward. "Come on, Robbie—let's go inside and get you dried off."

Kendall surrendered the child reluctantly, her heart touched by the way he clung to her. She looked up as Rick carried the boy toward the hotel, and the first thing she saw was the admiration glinting in Hawke's darkening gaze. Admiration and something else.

Softly, he asked, "Where did you learn that, Kendall?"

She glanced at the circle of inquiring faces and smiled brightly. "Well," she replied in an earnest, confiding tone, "I used to date a lifeguard. And he needed a *lot* of practice!"

It was the right thing to say. Laughing, the group broke up, most of them heading back into the hotel. Avoiding Hawke's thoughtful gaze, Kendall walked over to her cover-up —still lying on the tiles—and casually put it on.

"Father Thomas will want to thank you," Hawke said as he moved slowly toward her.

"Father Thomas?" She stepped into her thongs and reached to get her sunglasses and drop them into the beachbag.

"He runs the orphanage near here. Robbie's one of his kids."

Kendall felt her thinly healed wound throb in pain. Another orphan. Did it even the score somehow? she wondered dimly. One orphan had died because of her, and another had lived—because of her. Did it make up for . . . No. Nothing could ever make up for the loss of a precious life. Nothing . . .

"Kendall?"

She felt hands holding her shoulders in a gentle grip, and stared blankly up at Hawke's concerned face. "You've got that look in your eyes again," he said huskily. "That sad, hurting look. Kendall—"

Her eyes felt dry, scratchy. She wanted, suddenly, to cry. She wanted to throw herself on this man's broad chest and sob her heart out. But she couldn't. The tears were dammed up somewhere inside of her. Stepping back from him with fragile dignity, she clutched her beachbag firmly. "I think—that I'll go and lie down before dinner," she announced. "I'm very tired."

He didn't try to stop her or go with her, but Kendall could feel his eyes boring into her back all the way to the hotel doors. By the time she reached her room, she was in control again, although too tired to think about much of anything.

She took a shower and washed her hair, then slipped into a loose robe and went into the bedroom to find her dryer. Deliberately, she kept her mind blank while she dried her hair, unwilling to probe old wounds or wonder if she was about to acquire new ones.

Someone knocked on the door as she was putting the dryer away, and Kendall frowned as she checked her watch on the dresser. After five. She crossed the room to open the door, feeling her heart begin to beat unaccountably fast.

A red-jacketed waiter immediately swept in, propelling a small cart in front of him.

"But—I didn't order anything," Kendall protested blankly.

"Compliments of Mr. Madison, Miss James." The young waiter grinned engagingly as he gestured to the small plate of sandwiches and pitcher of iced tea on the cart. "He said to tell you that dinner would be served at eight downstairs."

Kendall didn't tell him that she'd read the hotel's brochure and knew very well when dinner would be served. She stepped closer to the cart and pointed to a small bowl. "And this?"

"Milk." The young man glanced rather warily at the spotted cat lying on the foot of the bed and staring at him balefully. "Mr. Madison sent it up for your cat."

"I see." She smiled at him sweetly. "Would you—express my appreciation to Mr. Madison, please?"

"Of course, Miss James." He started for the door.

"Just a minute—" Kendall reached for her purse, but the waiter was shaking his head.

"Mr. Madison took care of it, miss." He closed the door quietly behind him.

Kendall stared at the closed door for a moment, then looked wryly down at her cat. "Mr. Madison took care of it," she muttered to the extremely detached feline. "Gypsy, I think we're in trouble."

Two hours later, after the snack and a much-needed nap, Kendall stared at her closet indecisively. She wasn't sure that she wanted to brave the dining room. Room service would be safer. She had a rueful feeling that Hawke—with his talent for "taking care" of things—had probably arranged a cozy little table for two. Not that it was wise to assume anything where he was concerned. Still—the *safe* thing to do . . .

Kendall had never been one to opt for safety over possible danger. She was, her father had once told her irritably, positively reckless. Among other things.

The dress she chose was, ironically enough, one that she had fallen in love with for its illusory qualities. It was backless, strapless—and remained in place, apparently, by willpower and imagination. It defied every law of gravity and tended to spark some rather basic instincts in men. Kendall had always believed that the dress had been the cause of an Arabian sheikh's sudden desire to make a certain blond American his third wife.

Material as fine—and nearly as transparent—as a spider's

web cupped her full breasts lovingly and clung to the remainder of her body with a mind of its own. Beginning with a shade of gold almost exactly matching her tanned flesh, the material gradually darkened to the deep brown of the ankle-length hem. With every movement it shimmered and whispered seductively.

Closing her mind to the possible consequences of wearing such a dress, Kendall put her shoulder-length hair up in a smooth chignon, and then applied light makeup. She wore no jewelry, except for tiny diamond studs in her pierced ears.

She stood before the full-length mirror on the inside of the closet door for a moment and stared at her reflection. High-heeled sandals gave her added height and lent her an air of regal dignity. She thought, anyway. As for the dress . . . well, only time would tell if her decision to wear it had been prompted by sheer insanity.

She heard a knock at the door as she was dropping her room keys into a glittering evening purse. It might have been intuition, or just a built-in radar where he was concerned, but Kendall wasn't surprised to find Hawke leaning against the doorjamb. And—damn!—she might have known he'd look devastating in a dinner jacket.

Sternly commanding her senses to behave and her wits to remain sharp, she said brightly, "Well—this is what I call service. Have you come to escort me to dinner?"

"Yes . . ." His gray-eyed rapier glance moved slowly up

her body, settling at last on her inexplicably flushed face. "My God, but you're beautiful," he breathed huskily.

Kendall stared up at him for a moment, shaken not by what he had said but by the expression in his eyes. She had seen desire in a man's eyes before, but nothing like the naked wanting glowing in the shadowy depths of his gaze. And the fact that he made no effort to hide or disguise his desire disturbed her even more.

He would not, she realized then, play the gradual, gentle courtship game. He would not attempt to woo her with flowers and soft words and moonlight strolls. He intended to take what he wanted.

Kendall had a sudden cowardly impulse to fold up her tent and steal away. Fighting back the unfamiliar sensation, she swallowed hard and murmured, "Thank you," to the compliment.

He took her hand and drew her out into the hall, reaching to pull the door shut behind her. "And I," he added wryly, "will be the envy of every man in this hotel."

She made no effort to draw away when he continued to hold her hand and lead her down the wide hall, but she was beginning to feel rather as a fox must feel after hearing the sound of the huntmaster's horn.

"By the way—I haven't forgotten what happened by the pool."

"Did something happen by the pool?" she countered innocently, watching him press a button to summon the elevator as they reached the end of the hall.

"Something." He stared down at her a bit broodingly. "I haven't quite figured out what it was, but something definitely happened. I don't suppose you'd care to tell me why you nearly went into a trance after saving Robbie's life?"

"Shock." What was taking the elevator so long?

"No, it wasn't shock. In fact, you were in complete command of yourself. A bit surprising, that." One long finger stabbed the button again. "I would have expected you to panic —given your personality, that is."

"I think I've been insulted." Her voice was light, concealing the worry she felt. Stepping out of character by the pool had been a mistake, and Kendall was afraid that she would pay dearly for it. He was slightly suspicious of her innocent act now, and she had no idea how to allay those suspicions.

"Not at all." The elevator doors opened as he spoke, and Hawke led her into the car. Pressing the button for the lobby, he added coolly, "I was just making an observation. After all, honey, how many sweet, helpless women save lives without batting an eye?"

"It was—conditioned reflex, that's all." Kendall stared stonily at the closed doors, feeling the elevator begin to move smoothly downward. And then one of his hands cut across her line of sight, tapping a red button on the panel. The other hand

—still holding hers—pulled her abruptly close to him as the car stopped moving with a slight jerk.

The gray eyes laughed down at her as he carried her hand up to his shoulder and hauled her startled body fully against the hard length of his own. "What is there underneath all that innocence, Kendall?" he asked, a smoky darkness entering his eyes. "I have to find out."

"The—the elevator," she managed to protest, her fingers instinctively clutching the smooth white material covering his broad shoulder. "Someone may want it!"

"Let 'em take the stairs." His dark head bent, lips unerringly finding Kendall's in a kiss that sent shock waves surging through her body in an uncontrollable tide.

Never had a simple kiss affected her so strongly, and her much-vaunted sophistication went spinning off into nowhere. She was only vaguely aware of her hands creeping to tangle in the dark hair at his nape, felt small astonishment at the fact that she was returning his kiss. Warning bells were clanging loudly in her head, but Kendall ignored them.

His hands moved over her bare back, pulling her impossibly closer. Searing like a brand, his lips moved on hers, his tongue taking her mouth in a stunning surge of hunger. There was nothing gentle about the kiss, nothing tame. It was raw desire.

Kendall lost something in that moment. Her body recognized the touch of a master—*its* master—and all the defenses she had learned in a lifetime melted away. There was no rational thought in her mind to argue with her body's submission; a grinding need such as she had never known possessed her senses.

Hawke seemed to realize immediately that he had scored a point in this subtle game. He drew back only far enough to gaze down at her bemused face, his eyes darkened to some mysterious shade that Kendall found fascinating. "Unfortunately," he gritted softly, "this is not the time or the place. And I have a feeling that once I have you in my bed, I'll want to keep you there for a week."

It was not conscious intent that kept Kendall from completely abandoning her innocent pose—it was sheer panic. He was gazing down at her with an expression composed of desire and pure ownership, and, after what had just happened, Kendall had very little faith in her ability to hold him at arm's length.

She was caught, well and truly, between a rock and a hard place. Playing the innocent would leave her with almost no defense against Hawke's determination. And abandoning the charade would, she knew, arouse the hunter instinct in him.

Either way, Kendall had an awful feeling that she was going to end up right where he wanted her.

Putting off the moment of decision for as long as possible, she murmured, "Don't you think you're moving awfully fast?"

Keeping one arm around her, he reached to push the button that set the elevator in motion once again. "Not really." He sounded amused all at once. "As I said before—I don't have very much time where you're concerned."

"What if I don't like whirlwind romances?"

"I'll teach you to love them." He gave her a somewhat mocking glance.

Kendall felt suddenly that someone had hung a tag on her that proclaimed "sold" to all the world. And she didn't like it one damn bit. She would not—*would not*—admit that this man could master her! Hard on the heels of that resolve, the elevator doors hissed open, and she found herself staring at several obviously irritated hotel guests. The expressions—particularly the masculine ones—altered, though, to faint grins of amusement.

Fighting an absurd desire to look down and make sure that the symbolic tag she had visualized hadn't suddenly materialized, Kendall gave them back stare for stare and sedately accompanied Hawke from the elevator. Her coloring didn't betray her, but she was blushing vividly inside.

He led her through the lobby, not, apparently, the least bit disturbed either by Kendall's silence or by the knowing looks that followed them. Keeping an arm casually around her shoulders, he led her down a side hall to the tremendous dining room.

Kendall looked around interestedly as Hawke stopped to have a word with the headwaiter. She had known from the moment of entering it that this was a classy hotel; the dining room was ample evidence of that fact. The glittering formal room could quite easily have hosted a presidential ball.

Although the majority of her travels had been spent in various third world countries, Kendall was no stranger to glamour. She could remember nightly parties in diplomatic colonies where there had been conversation in six languages and decorations sprinkled across dinner jackets. It had been a part of her father's profession that she had always loved—no matter how many times he'd groused about having to deal with diplomats and bureaucrats.

And this room was . . . Kendall suddenly caught sight of her reflection in the mirrored archway leading into the dining room, and knew immediately why the guests in the lobby had grinned knowingly. She looked as if she'd just been kissed—and very thoroughly too. Her blue-green eyes were dark and disturbed, her mouth tremulous and bearing a faintly bruised look—and her lipstick was slightly smeared.

It was the jolt she needed to snap her out of her state of uncharacteristic meekness.

With vast self-control Kendall reached up to carefully erase the pink smear. Her blue-green eyes took on a shuttered expression in the mirror. Her decision had been made. Out of her depth or not, she wasn't going to give in to Hawke Madison without one hell of a fight.

With outward serenity she followed the waiter across the

large room . . . to a cozy little table for two. Terrific. Taking the chair that was pulled out for her, she accepted a menu and smiled sweetly at the waiter. Looking across the table at Hawke, she said, "Why don't you order for me."

"Delighted." He smiled at her.

Of course. Kendall propped her elbows on the table, lacing her fingers together and resting her chin on them as she gazed steadily across the table at Hawke with what she devoutly hoped was an unreadable expression. Shoving the episode in the elevator out of her mind, she tuned out Hawke's voice and considered, very sanely, what she was about to do.

There was nothing simple about it. For the first time in her life Kendall felt a need to prove herself. If Hawke turned out to be the stronger of the two of them, the result would be more than just a summer fling. There was a very good chance, she admitted silently, that she would leave her heart behind when she left paradise. She was shrewd enough—and honest enough —to realize that she could easily fall in love with this man.

That was point one. Point two was even more complicated. No matter how innocent and helpless she had pretended to be, Kendall had never yet allowed herself to be dominated. And Hawke had looked at her, only moments before, with pure possession in his eyes. She would not become his toy.

It could, indeed, very well become the clash of the Titans. And devil take the hindmost.

"You're staring at me." He sounded amused.

Kendall blinked and focused on the man across from her. "So I am. Aren't you flattered?"

His gray eyes narrowed, and Hawke leaned back in his chair to stare at her consideringly. "Somehow I get the feeling that you are not the same lady who got off the elevator with me."

She wet her index finger with the tip of her tongue and made an imaginary mark in the air. "Give the man a cigar," she said in a mocking tone.

Surprisingly, an expression of immense satisfaction spread across his lean face. "I was right, then; you aren't nearly the brainless blonde you pretend to be."

"Never fooled you for a moment, in fact."

"For a moment—yes. But only for a moment. I had a feeling that you were going to turn out to be something special, honey."

She smiled coolly, her manner as different from the pose of sweet innocence as night from day. "I told you before, Hawke; I'm not interested in a summer romance. So if you're thinking of carving another notch on your gun, forget it."

He looked wounded. "How crude."

"But true." Kendall gestured vaguely at the glitter and glamour surrounding them. "Your business is charm, Hawke; we both know that. The majority of your guests are women, and the majority of your staff are handsome, charming men. A very—restful place for a frustrated soul, wouldn't you say?"

"And are you?"

"What?" she asked, knowing the answer.

"Frustrated."

"No." Her voice was amused. "That's never been one of my problems." She sat back to allow an approaching waiter to place their meal on the table, realizing that her remark could easily be taken the wrong way, but not really concerned about it. When the waiter had left, she picked up her spoon to begin on the soup.

Picking up his own spoon, Hawke said conversationally, "None of that changes my mind, you know. But we'll get back to that later. Tell me, Kendall—why the charade?"

"Why not?" She looked at him wryly. "I am what people expect me to be."

"You mean men."

"Sure. Oh, I could rant and rave about not being valued for who I am instead of what I look like, but what good would that do? My way is much easier. And there's no harm done."

"I don't know about that." Seriously, he went on. "By being what people expect you to be, you don't give anyone the chance to see the real you."

Interested in spite of herself, she frowned thoughtfully. "But how many people really care what's beneath the surface, Hawke? Not many," she went on, answering her own question. "We all act out roles we've given ourselves, pretend to be things we're not—or things we want to be. And we build walls around things we want to hide."

"What do you want to hide, Kendall?" he asked softly.

Ignoring the question, she continued calmly. "It's human nature. We want to guess everyone else's secrets without giving our own away."

"And if someone wants to see beneath the surface?"

Kendall shrugged. "We make them dig for it. You know— make them prove themselves worthy of our trust. Of all the animals on this earth, we're the most suspicious of a hand held out in friendship."

Hawke pushed his bowl away and gazed at her with an oddly sober gleam in his eye. "Sounds like you learned that lesson the hard way," he commented quietly.

She stared at him, surprise in her eyes, realizing for the first time just how cynical she'd become. Obeying some name-less command in his smoky eyes, she said slowly, "I've seen too much to be innocent, Hawke. Whatever ideals I had . . . died long ago."

He stared at her for a moment, then murmured, "I think I'd better find a pick and a shovel."

Suddenly angry with her own burst of self-revelation, Kendall snapped irritably, "Why?"

"To dig beneath the surface." He smiled slowly. "You're a fascinating lady, Kendall James. And I think . . . if I dig deep enough . . . I just might find gold."

"What you might find," she warned coolly, "is a booby trap. I'm not a puzzle to be solved, Hawke."

"Aren't you? You act the sweet innocent, telling yourself that it's the easy way. And it's a good act, very convincing and probably very useful. But it isn't entirely an act, is it, honey? There is an innocent inside of you, hiding from the things she's seen."

"You're not a psychologist and I'm not a patient, so stop with the analyzing," she muttered, trying to ignore what he was saying.

"You're a romantic, an idealist," he went on as if she hadn't spoken. "But you hide that part of your nature—behind a wall that isn't a wall at all. You've got yourself convinced that it's an act, and that conviction keeps you from being hurt."

Kendall shot him a glare from beneath her lashes. "Now you're not even making sense," she retorted scornfully.

"Oh, yes, I am." His eyes got that hooded look she was beginning to recognize out of sheer self-defense. "A piece of the puzzle just fell into place. But it's still a long way from being solved. And, rest assured, Kendall, I intend to solve it."

"Is this in the nature of another warning?" she asked lightly, irritated that her heart had begun to beat like a jungle drum.

"Call it anything you like."

"I could just leave, you know."

"You could." The heavy lids lifted, revealing a cool challenge. "But that would be cowardly."

Knowing—*knowing*—that she was walking right into his trap, Kendall snapped, "I'm a lot of things, Hawke, but a coward isn't one of them!" And she felt strongly tempted to throw her soup bowl at him when she saw the satisfaction that flickered briefly in his eyes.

"Good," he said briskly. "Then we can forget about that angle, can't we? And get down to business."

"Business?" she asked wryly. "That's one I haven't heard."

"Well, I would have called it romance, but I didn't want you to laugh at me." He grinned faintly. "Men are more romantic than women, you know. I read it somewhere."

"Fancy that." Kendall stared at him. "Most of the men I've known let romance go by the board."

"Really? Then knowing me will be an education."

An hour later, strolling with Hawke along a moonlit beach, she had to admit that she'd gotten her signals crossed where he was concerned. Either that, or else he was playing a very deep game. She had an odd feeling that Hawke himself had abruptly decided to change his game plan sometime during dinner.

For the past hour he'd been the perfect companion. After dinner he'd invited her for a stroll on the beach, and ever since then he'd talked casually about various things. Politics. Sports. The weather.

It made Kendall *extremely* nervous.

Gently freeing herself from the light grip of his fingers, Kendall walked to the edge of the water. Having shed her sandals earlier, she held up her long skirt with one hand and let the warm water lap against her feet. She had always loved the sight of a full moon hanging low over the ocean and, for some reason, tonight's moon was even more beautiful than usual.

She half turned, intending to make some remark to Hawke, but the words never left her throat. He was standing only a couple of feet away, staring at her with an intensity that was both frightening and strangely compelling.

"What does it feel like, Kendall?" he asked with unexpected roughness, his voice barely audible over the muted roar of the surf.

"What does what feel like?" She had to swallow hard before the words would emerge properly.

"Living inside that body, behind that face. Knowing that the world stops when you walk by." The deep, gritty voice had taken on some quality Kendall couldn't put a name to. Still. Waiting.

She felt, strangely, that this moment was somehow important, but she didn't know why. And she didn't know how to respond to his words. "Don't—be ridiculous."

"How does it feel?" he insisted softly, stepping closer.

Yet again, something in his gray eyes seemed to draw a response from deep inside of her. "It feels like a curse," she whispered, hearing an unfamiliar pain in her voice. "And a cage . . ."

He reached out suddenly, enfolding her in his arms. It seemed to be a comforting embrace, and Kendall accepted it as such. She rested her cheek against his chest, hearing the heavy beat of his heart and feeling bewildered.

"What are you doing to me?" she pleaded softly.

"Introducing you to the real Kendall," he responded almost gently, his lips moving in a feather caress against her hair. "I think you lost her somewhere along the way."

"I don't understand."

"I'm digging." His voice was whimsical. "And I'm going to go on digging until I find the real Kendall. And for the first time in your life, you're going to face your own emotions."

Kendall thought briefly of what had happened in South America, and her iron control since then, but brushed the memory away. Trying to infuse her voice with lightness, she mocked softly, "Fascinating! So what did the first few shovelfuls uncover, Sherlock?"

His arms tightened slightly when she would have drawn away. In a considering tone, he replied, "The fact that you feel trapped inside yourself. You use your beauty—deliberately, consciously—because it's easier that way, and because there's really very little you can do about it anyway. But you hate always being taken at face value. And you've convinced yourself that no one ever takes the time or the trouble to look beneath the surface."

"What an awful lot you've uncovered," she mused dryly, trying again to free herself and giving up again when he refused to release her. *"Are* you a psychologist, by any chance?"

"No. Should I hang out a shingle?"

"If you think I'm going to answer that, you're crazy!"

"That's all right, honey." His voice was cheerful. "By the time I've finished, you'll admit that I'm right."

"Oh, really?" Kendall's father would have beaten a hasty retreat after hearing that tone. Hawke, apparently, didn't see the warning signs flashing in neon.

"Sure. You go right on acting; it's fine with me. It'll keep other men at a distance. In the meantime, I'll just go right on digging. If it takes the rest of my life, Miss James, I'm going to uncover all your secrets."

Kendall wasn't so angry that she didn't feel a trace of panic. Cheerful or not, he sounded utterly sure of himself, and obviously meant exactly what he said. She needed time to think, to plan some defense.

That time wasn't granted.

Hawke bent his head, nuzzling the soft, sensitive skin just beneath her ear. "Of course," he murmured huskily, "I may detour now and then from the subject at hand."

Kendall fought off an attack of dizziness and struggled to

make her voice cool and even. "I think I'd better warn you, Hawke—I'm not any more helpless physically than I am mentally."

"Picked up a few tricks along the way, eh?" His voice was softly amused, his breath warm in her ear.

"A few. And they are—so I've been told—acutely painful." Judging by the traitorously weakened state of her muscles at that moment, Kendall wasn't sure that she could even attempt any of those nasty little tricks. He didn't have to know that though.

He chuckled deep in his chest, his mouth concentrating on the pulse beating frantically at the base of her neck. "Brute strength usually wins out, honey. Besides—we don't want to turn this into a battle of muscles. Unfair tactics."

"And *this* isn't an unfair tactic?" It was almost a wail of desperation, and she hated herself for the betraying uncertainty. She could feel the pounding of the surf enter her bloodstream, sapping her will, hear his heart begin to beat with an unsteady rhythm.

"It's the only edge I have," he gritted suddenly, lifting his head and staring down at her. "I want you, Kendall."

"But I don't want you!" she lied stoutly.

The dark head swooped, his mouth capturing lips parted to form another protest. Another useless protest. There was something greedy in his kiss, sparking an answering hunger within her.

Kendall was only dimly aware that he had taken the purse and sandals from her nerveless fingers and tossed them on the beach. She felt herself crushed against his broad chest, senses going crazy and rational thought shattering like glass. Something that had slumbered peacefully inside of her for years awoke suddenly.

Her hands slid beneath his unbuttoned jacket and around to feel the rippling muscles in his back. She felt one of his hands pulling her lower body fiercely against his, and the heat of his desire burned and seduced. Mindlessly, she clung to his strength, her tongue joining his in a duel.

She didn't care that she was giving herself away beyond any chance of denial. The only thing that mattered to her at that moment was the satisfaction of this nameless need.

Hawke tore his mouth from hers suddenly, gazing down at her with gray eyes gone almost black with desire. "Oh, no?"

C h a p t e r

4

For one brief, insane moment, Kendall didn't understand the harsh words. She stared up at him bemusedly, vaguely noting that the moonlight lent his face an air of stark aggression that was just slightly short of alarming. And then she realized that the moonlight had very little to do with it . . . which was *nothing* short of alarming.

Sanity rushed in to fill the cold void left by that realization, and with it temper. Damn! What was the man—a sorcerer? What *was* he that he could do this to her?

She tried fiercely to break away from him, and discovered his grip to be as immovable as the island they stood on. *"Animals* can be attracted to one another," she snapped witheringly, pushing against his broad chest with both hands and achieving no very noticeable result. "It doesn't mean a thing."

"Doesn't it?" Like a lumbering bear ignoring the puppy snapping at its heels, Hawke ignored her efforts to escape. "It means that you want me, Kendall—and that's enough to start with."

She stopped struggling suddenly, and lifted her chin with fiery dignity. Bright moonlight showed clearly the anger glittering in her blue-green eyes. "Be that as it may," she shot back coldly, "I have no intention of getting involved with you. And if that means I'll have to leave this island—then I will. Cowardly or not."

Apparently realizing that goading her would serve no useful purpose this time, he stared down at her for a moment. "Then I'll make a deal with you," he told her in a very neutral voice.

In spite of herself Kendall asked, "What kind of deal?"

"You don't run away, and I won't—force my attentions on you."

"There's a clinker in there somewhere." She stared at him suspiciously, trying to forget that his arms were still around her and his hands burning against her bare back. "What exactly do you mean by that?"

"Nothing sinister. In fact, it's really very simple. You have the control, Kendall. I intend to make love to you at every opportunity—we both know that. But you hold the reins. I give you my word that I'll stop when you say to."

Kendall knew that she was a fool to even consider his "deal," but she didn't see any other choice. She couldn't go back to South America, and she couldn't leave the resort because her father was to meet her here. Surely she had enough control to hold Hawke at arm's length! Besides that . . . she had never in her life run away from a fight.

And there was something exhilarating in the thought that she would have a special power in this relationship. Rather like a lion tamer must feel . . . because he had the gun.

It was the reckless Kendall who spoke, while the worried little voice inside her head moaned a warning. "Will you keep your word, Hawke?"

"I swear. I won't force you into a thing."

Well, Kendall knew, there was force . . . and then there was *force*. A small distinction with dangerous possibilities. But as the tension flowed from her body, she knew that the decision had been made. It was a new game now, with new rules. And the biggest rule of all depended on her own self-control. "All right—I agree."

The gray eyes took on that unnervingly satisfied gleam again, and Kendall wondered what she'd gotten herself into. "Good," he stated softly.

She tried cautiously to disentangle herself from his hold. "I'd like to go back to the hotel now, Hawke. It's been a long day, and I'm tired."

For a moment she thought he would ignore the request. But then he sighed heavily and stepped back, his arms falling away from her. "All right, honey—if that's what you want." He bent to pick up her purse and sandals from the sand, and added humorously, "I'm afraid the hem of your dress is wet."

"So are your shoes." She was grateful for the lightness that had replaced the turbulent emotions of passion and anger. Unobtrusively, she tugged at the bodice of her dress, realizing ruefully that the wet hem was acting as weight to pull down the material. If she were lucky, she just might make it back to the hotel without disgracing herself. If not—well, she could always borrow Hawke's jacket. . . .

It was a giddy thought. A moment later Hawke had turned abruptly back to her, picked her up as easily as though she were a child, and began striding along the beach toward the hotel.

"Hawke!"

"Well, you're barefooted," he explained reasonably, her slight weight obviously not disturbing him in the least.

Kendall clutched his neck instinctively. "You have my sandals! Put me down, and I'll—"

"You'll never get all the sand off your feet. And I'm sure you know how uncomfortable it is to walk in sandy shoes."

"I'll bear up. Hawke, for heaven's sake! What if someone sees this caveman display?"

"People expect to see this sort of thing here. I started to name this place the Love Resort, you know, but changed my mind. Too sappy."

Kendall ignored the information. Feeling her dress slip a

bit more, she said irritably, "I thought you said I could call a halt—"

"This isn't lovemaking," he cut her off ruthlessly in a bland voice. "It's romancing. Haven't you ever read the part where the heroine gets swept off her feet?"

In all the books Kendall had read, the heroine got swept off her feet and right into the hero's bed. "Now, look," she began, but broke off hastily as they encountered another couple on leaving the beach and starting up the path to the hotel.

Polite words were exchanged between Hawke and the other man, and the four passed one another. As the other couple stepped onto the beach and she and Hawke started to round a curve on the path, Kendall distinctly heard the young woman say enviously to her escort, "How sweet! Why aren't you ever that romantic?"

In spite of herself, Kendall giggled. Reading the gleam of laughter in the glance Hawke slanted her way, she recovered quickly and said, "Don't think that excuses you. Just because it's her idea of romance doesn't mean it's mine."

"You mean it's not?" He didn't seem noticeably dashed.

"No," she lied, thinking of knights on white chargers and outmoded chivalry. And dodos and dinosaurs. They had all been killed by the times. "Aren't you getting tired?" she asked with hope, knowing that it would be futile to struggle and that she would appear as helpless as a three-day-old kitten if she tried.

"Not at all—you're as light as a feather."

They emerged from the path into the well-lighted pool area just then, and Kendall felt a flush rise in her cheeks as she blinked and encountered the interested stares from two late-night swimmers. One of the women asked the other in an envious stage-whisper, "Does he do that for all his guests?" And the other answered sadly, "Only the lucky ones."

Kendall giggled again, and then realized that they were nearly at the hotel door. "Hawke!" she whispered fiercely, tugging on his ear to get his attention. It seemed an absurd thing to do, but she was feeling giddy again. "Put me down this instant! You can't carry me through the hotel lobby!"

"Why not?"

Why not, indeed. Without the slightest sign of embarrassment, he carried her through the lobby. Unfortunately, at least half the guests in the hotel seemed to be milling around in the lobby. At least, it seemed so to Kendall, although there were probably only a dozen or so people. As if that made a difference.

Conscious of her bare, sand-covered feet, damp dress, and windblown hair, Kendall resolutely kept her gaze fixed on the rather formidable angle of Hawke's jaw. She heard a couple of giggles and literally *felt* several grins, but she didn't look up. And it didn't help that they had to wait several minutes for the elevator . . . which delivered another half dozen witnesses.

When the elevator doors at last hissed shut behind them,

Kendall glanced around guardedly and found that they were alone. And found Hawke gazing down at her with a purely male grin and laughter dancing in his eyes.

"I don't suppose," she said carefully, "that anyone down there thought you were being heroic to an accident victim? A sprained ankle or something?"

"I doubt it."

"And I don't suppose you'd care to explain to them that this is not what it looks like?"

"No," he answered simply, the grin still present.

"Uh-huh." Kendall felt an insane urge to burst out laughing. "I'll have to get busy tonight."

"Doing what?"

"Embroidering scarlet A's on all my blouses."

Hawke laughed softly as he leaned against the wall of the elevator. "How does it feel to be a scarlet woman?"

"Embarrassing. Tell me"—she linked her fingers together at the back of his neck—"should I expect more of this sort of thing?"

"It's romance," he protested, wounded.

"Oh, so *that's* what you call it. I never would have guessed."

"You really love it."

She sighed. "People with egos like yours should be locked up. Were you born self-confident, or was it just a little something you learned along the way?"

"Inherited. Just ask my mother."

The elevator doors opened before Kendall could frame an adequate response. Having learned the uselessness of protest, she remained silent as Hawke carried her down the hall.

He stopped at the door of her room and lifted a quizzical eyebrow. "Your key?"

"It's in my purse," she informed him politely. "Which I trust you still have."

"So I do. A bit awkward, though." He looked up the hall as a door opened, then smiled as a red-jacketed young man emerged pushing a serving cart. "Mike," he called out, "would you give us a hand here?"

"Of course, Mr. Madison." Mike stopped the cart near them and chastely averted his eyes from Kendall's bare feet, looking at his employer with a poker face that did credit to his control. "How can I help?"

"Miss James's door key—would you get it out of the purse, please, and unlock the door?" Hawke looked at Kendall with belated, mocking concern. "You don't mind, do you, honey?"

"Of *course* not." Whether it was giddiness or sheer resignation, Kendall felt extremely detached from the moment. So what if her reputation was shot to hell? She hoped none of these people moved in the same circles as a mining engineer, so if she could whisk her father away quick enough, he need never know.

Mike located the key in Kendall's purse and unlocked the door, then swung it open, replaced the key, and solemnly handed the purse to her. Kendall murmured an absurd thank-you, and wondered vaguely if Hawke had planned the whole damn scene.

"Thanks, Mike." Hawke watched as the young man continued down the hall with his cart, then smiled down at Kendall. "It's nice to have a helping hand now and then," he commented.

"Are you dead to all shame?" she asked with the objective interest of someone searching for the answer to a somewhat puzzling question.

"Not at all." He carried her into her room—leaving the door open—and set her gently on the foot of the bed, dropping the sandals at her feet. "Now . . . does madam require anything else?"

Kendall stared at him a little wildly. "A psychiatrist and a couch. I must be out of my mind."

"My couch is vacant at the moment." Somehow, he managed to leer with his eyebrows.

"Thanks—I'll pass." She could have added that having already experienced the effectiveness of his "couch," she wasn't eager to repeat the less-than-fun experience.

"Anything else I can do to help?" He looked ridiculously hopeful. "If you'd care to soak in a hot tub, I'll be glad to wash your back for you. Or anything else—"

"Never mind," she interrupted a little desperately. "I get the picture! Thanks, but no thanks." She made a sudden grab at the top of her dress as it gave up the ghost and decided to obey the laws of gravity. "If you'd just leave—?"

Hawke grinned, interestedly watching her struggle with the dress. "Need any help with your zipper?" he asked innocently.

If Kendall hadn't been afraid of losing the battle with her dress, she would have thrown her purse at him. "Just—leave!"

Hawke bowed with stilted dignity and backed toward the door, obviously intent on watching the unintended strip-scene for as long as possible. "If you need anything—anything at all—"

"I'll whistle, shall I?" She glared at him, trying not to let the bubble of laughter in her throat escape.

"Or call room service—they'll pass the message along."

"Hawke!"

"See you in the morning, honey." He laughed, then closed the door quietly behind him.

Kendall stared at the closed door for a moment, absently releasing the grip on her dress and allowing the material to find its own level. She thought of laughter and romance, of fragile ideals and cherished illusions. She thought of paradise, and knights riding by on white chargers and moonlight. She thought of a bruised and weary heart with too many good-byes engraved on it, and an optimism bruised from too many head-on collisions with reality.

She thought of charades and other games. Like this one—where romance was the key and the stakes were high—very high. And the joker was wild. Speaking to the man who could no longer hear her, she mused vaguely, "But in your game, Hawke . . . the *game* is wild."

She glanced absently at the balcony door to see Gypsy emerge and favor her with a disapproving stare. "Gypsy, we are *definitely* in trouble!"

Muted thunder woke her up the next morning, and Kendall moaned sleepily and pulled the pillow around her ears to shut out the sound. It didn't help, though, and she muttered irritably for someone to kill the noisy intruder. It was a moment before she identified the sound as someone pounding on her door.

Still more than half asleep, she flung back the covers and pulled herself from the bed, feeling almost blindly around for her robe and slippers and finding neither. Deciding to hell with it, she made her way to the door, more by a terrific sense of direction than anything else, and flung it open. The glare on her face—sleepy though it was—should have curled somebody's hair.

Except that it didn't.

Hawke returned the glare as he leaned against the jamb, one hand holding an indignantly struggling Gypsy by the scruff of her neck. "It's about time!" he snapped, obviously not in the best of moods.

Kendall focused on the rather odd scene in front of her, and grasped one important fact. "What are you doing with my cat?" she demanded with early-morning temper.

"It isn't love of her company, believe me." His voice was carefully restrained. "In fact, I've been tempted to drown her. I just fished her out of the couple next door's bathtub. They are not happy. And since they requested the honeymoon suite because they understandably wanted privacy, I don't blame them."

"Gypsy likes water," Kendall defended her pet, again grasping only the relevant fact.

"She also likes chewing on various parts of the human anatomy, as one very unhappy hotel employee can attest to. Either put her in a cage, Kendall, or make damn sure she doesn't get out of your room at night. The last thing I need is a lawsuit!"

"I will not put Gypsy in a cage!" The logical part of Kendall's mind realized that her cat must have loosened the leash and leapt from her balcony to the one next door. The same little compartment of her mind also noted that Hawke had apparently dressed in a hurry without taking the time to shave. But, having been rudely awakened after lying awake for most of the night, Kendall was in no mood to heed the logical voice warning her to be conciliatory.

"Then put a leash on her." Hawke ignored the cat's attempts to scratch him. His glare faded suddenly as his gray eyes dropped to take in her petite figure, clothed only in baby-doll pajamas so sheer that it hardly seemed worth the effort.

Unaware that his mood was rapidly changing, Kendall reached out to grab her pet. She held the cat against her breast securely, glaring at Hawke and totally unconscious of the fact that the wet animal was bringing her pajamas one step closer to invisibility. "I did leash her!" she snapped.

"Well . . . try to keep her in your room, then, and not on the balcony." It was an almost absent request, delivered in a deepening voice as his eyes continued to rove almost hungrily over her. "Dammit, Kendall—do you own a single outfit that *isn't* sexy?"

The sudden demand startled Kendall, and woke her up with a vengeance. Clutching her cat, she stared at him warily, remembering the bargain struck the night before. Dumb. Oh, she had been dumb! Trying to save a hopeless situation, she told him calmly, "My clothes are none of your business."

It was damnably hard to be dignified when one was barefoot, wearing skimpy pajamas, and clutching a wet cat, but Kendall gave it her best shot. And Hawke, devil that he was, changed moods on her again.

With a sudden grin he said softly, "I loved the slippery dress last night, but this is even better."

Kendall felt definitely hunted when an older woman passed by the doorway just in time to hear Hawke's remark and tossed a startled, somewhat amused glance at Kendall. Resigned, Kendall recognized one of the women who had been by the pool the night before.

Did he *plan* these encounters, for God's sake, or was she simply incredibly unlucky? Twenty-five years with a spotless reputation, and everything changed overnight. The thought roused a justifiable anger. "If you *don't* mind, I'd like to go back to bed," she said stiffly, realizing too late that her word choice had not been the best.

"I don't mind at all." He took a step inside the room, gray eyes glittering with laughter and something else. "In fact, I'd say that it was a perfect way to start the day."

For a panicky moment Kendall felt almost overwhelmed by the hypnotic gray eyes. And then Gypsy solved the problem by swiping angrily at Hawke with a set of very impressive claws.

Forced to step back again or be branded for life, Hawke stared at the cat a bit ominously. "You," he informed the irritated feline, "ought to be shot."

Unimpressed, Gypsy growled low in her throat and attempted another swipe. Smiling sweetly, Kendall closed the door gently in Hawke's bemused face.

Securely latching the balcony door, Kendall released her

pet and then tried to recapture sleep. It didn't work, of course. She had shed the damp pajamas, thinking wrathfully that if anyone—unnamed—woke her up again, there *would* be a show. But sleep eluded her.

Giving up after half an hour, she rose once again and took a shower, then dressed in cutoff jeans and a short-sleeved cotton shirt, tied at her waist. Slipping her feet into a pair of thongs, she found her purse. Automatically checking her wallet, she dropped her room key inside. She had to get away from the hotel for a while.

It wasn't so much a conscious decision as a need. Absently, she found Gypsy's food and water dishes, filled one with water and the other with some of the dry food she'd bought in Nassau the day before, and placed both dishes by the locked balcony door.

A few moments later she was leaving the elevator in the lobby, and hoping that Hawke was nowhere around. Since it was fairly early for most of the guests, the lobby was silent, and Kendall hurried toward the doors.

"Miss James?"

She halted and turned to face Rick Evans. "Mr. Evans." Her voice was resigned. "Is something wrong?"

"No, of course not." He looked a little uncertain as he reached her, his smile tentative. "It's just—Miss James, would you mind very much changing rooms?"

She looked surprised, and he hurried on to explain.

"There was a mixup in our reservations, and one of the guests who requested two rooms on your floor has only one. He's arrived earlier than expected, and since he's a regular guest . . ."

Kendall smiled faintly. "I don't mind at all. Shall I move my things now, or—"

"The staff will move everything for you, if that's all right. I can see you're on your way out." He grinned slightly. "I may have to roust Hawke to move the cat, but I'm sure he won't mind."

Thinking of Hawke grappling with Gypsy's temperamental nature gave the news an added plus as far as Kendall was concerned. Smiling, she handed over her key and accepted the one held out to her.

"It's a suite on the top floor," the manager elaborated, "but there's no extra charge. I'm sorry for the inconvenience, Miss James."

"No trouble," she said politely. Dropping the key into her purse, she waved cheerily and then hastily made good her escape before Hawke could pop out of nowhere and create another embarrassing situation out of thin air.

Emerging into the early-morning sunlight, Kendall had no very clear idea of where she was going. She looked thoughtfully at the two cabs parked outside the hotel entrance and flipped a mental coin, then began walking.

The village was easy to locate, and she wandered down the

shaded streets and window-shopped for an hour or so. Some-time later her steps slowed as she followed the path toward the dignified old church not far from the hotel. She could hear the laughter and shrieks of children at play, and the sound stopped her dead in her tracks.

She loved children and emotionally had adopted kids all over the world. It was always painful to leave them behind when her father was transferred and they moved on again.

Her father had warned her years before that she would tear herself apart over "her kids." He had used it as an argu-ment for settling down and having kids of her own, telling her that one day she would love a child too much, and be heart-broken at the inevitable parting.

It hadn't worked out that way though—it had been the other way around. The child she had loved had left her, and Kendall was desperately afraid to become attached to another.

"May I help you?"

Startled, she focused on an elderly man whose gentle brown eyes and serene expression gave her a very good idea who he was. The collar helped. "Father Thomas?"

"Yes." The eyes moved over her in an unexpectedly shrewd inspection. "You're Miss James."

"Kendall," she corrected him automatically, her surprise obvious. "But how did you know?"

He smiled. "Hawke brought Robbie back from the hotel

yesterday afternoon and explained what had happened. I have to thank you, Kendall. If it hadn't been for you—"

"Please." Kendall smiled a little shakily, thrown by this man's friendship with Hawke, although she didn't know why. "If I hadn't been there, someone else would have helped." Another happy shriek drew her eyes irresistibly to the square whitewashed building behind the church. "Father—if you don't mind, I'd like to spend some time with the children."

"Of course, Kendall." Smiling, he led the way to the surprisingly well-equipped playground between the church and the orphanage. Seeing Kendall's expression, the priest explained, "Hawke provides a few extras for the children."

Kendall didn't want to hear that. Not that she wanted to deprive the children, but everything she heard about Hawke seemed to produce yet another bond between them, and that was the last thing she needed. She didn't have time to worry over it, though, because she was surrounded by laughing children a moment later.

As always, Kendall lost track of time as she played with the kids. When lunchtime came, Father Thomas invited her to stay, and she did. But she almost regretted it when the priest spent the whole time talking about Hawke. Interested, and yet troubled by the certainty that she was becoming involved with Hawke in spite of herself, Kendall listened.

Father Thomas spoke of his younger friend with great affection and respect. He told Kendall that Hawke had been decorated several times in Vietnam—something the priest had learned through a mutual friend, since Hawke didn't talk about it—and wounded once while evacuating children from a small hospital under enemy fire. He told her about Hawke's intelligence, his sensitivity, his concern for the people around him.

Kendall listened, her first impression of Hawke as a hard man fading away. And that, she knew, was dangerous. Knowing it did nothing to change it. Father Thomas drew a vivid picture of a man who felt more than he showed, who had seen—like Kendall—too much to be innocent. A man with chinks in his armor.

It was late in the afternoon when Kendall left the orphanage, thanking Father Thomas and receiving his assurances that she was welcome anytime.

Instead of walking directly back to the hotel, Kendall wandered slowly along a path until she came to the rocky cliffs on the north end of the island. She picked her way carefully, recognizing the area from her brief flight over the island in the small plane that had brought her from Nassau. Moving south, she reached a point where she could see the hotel in the distance, and look down from the cliffs to the beginnings of the sandy beach she and Hawke had walked the night before.

Kendall sat down a foot from the edge, deciding vaguely to watch the sunset. But her thoughts occupied her, thoughts she had pushed aside after lunch with Father Thomas.

Hugging her knees, she listened to the roar of the surf and

her thoughts. She had enjoyed the past fifteen years, the good times far outweighing the bad. But she felt . . . so weary. Not a physical weariness, but an emotional one. She had never known roots. The most stable thing in her life was her father's love, and she had always lived with the knowledge that her father could be killed without warning.

It had made each moment precious, perhaps explaining her need to travel with him. But she couldn't cling to her father forever. She was independent physically and mentally—but emotionally, the child inside her had not yet learned to trust other relationships. The child clung to its father as the only solid thing in a painful world.

Kendall knew herself. And she knew that it was time for her to let go of her father. His life was not hers. Her life was . . . what? Undiscovered, as yet.

It was a peculiar moment. She felt almost reborn. And scared. So scared. But several things were clear to her. She would no longer pretend—with anyone. The useful and easily assumed dumb blonde was gone forever. Hawke had been right; she was cheating herself, and others, by presenting a bland appearance to the world.

It was astonishingly clear to her. She wasn't quite sure why. But instinct told her that it had a great deal to do with Hawke. It was one subject she wanted to shy away from, but Kendall forced herself to face it.

Because that was clear too. Hawke was important in her

life. A man she had known just over twenty-four hours. She still intended to fight any physical relationship, but her reasons were different now. Before, she had wanted to avoid any relationship. Cut and dried. But now she knew that that was impossible. She was drawn to him mentally as well as physically. The relationship—however it could be defined—existed.

But Kendall would not commit herself. Not yet. If she had seen too much to be innocent, then she had also seen how brief and uncertain life really was. It was not a pessimistic thought, but a calm understanding. If she gave her body, she would give her heart. And she would be very, very sure. Love was too precious to waste.

All at once she was vividly aware of the roar of the surf, the sun hanging low in a burning sky, the smell of the salty sea crashing against the rocks below her. And a new sense told her that he was coming. She wondered dimly at the sensation and what it indicated.

"Kendall?" His voice was quiet, almost hushed, as though the weight of her thoughts had touched him. He sat down beside her. "I was worried about you."

"You have no right to worry." Immediately, she wished that she could recall the shrewish words, but he seemed undisturbed.

"No, I suppose not. Still—I was worried. You shouldn't wander around on these cliffs."

Kendall rested her chin on her knees and stared out at the

dying sun. "I've climbed mountains in Europe." It wasn't a boastful statement. Just a statement.

"Really? Did you enjoy it?" He was serious, not mocking.

Kendall flicked a glance at him, and felt a glimmer of humor lighten her somber mood. "No. Our guide had a bit too much out of his flask the third day out and dropped half our equipment over a ledge. That was the first climb. On the second climb, it rained for four miserable days, and I developed pneumonia. Needless to say, I gave up climbing."

"You've had an adventurous life, it seems."

"Very." She hesitated, then went on, compelled by his presence or by the curious twilight between day and night. Her voice was calm and contemplative. "I've attended coronations and diplomatic balls. Ridden camels and elephants. Watched oil fires and revolutions. I've hiked through jungles and deserts. I've seen a world the tourists will never see."

His head turned slightly, Hawke had watched her profile intently while she spoke. "And now?" he asked quietly.

Kendall felt an odd jolt somewhere inside her. Was it just a simple coincidence that he had asked precisely the question she had asked herself? *And now . . . what?* She shivered.

Immediately, Hawke rose to his feet and extended a hand to help her up. He stood for a moment, still holding her hand as he stared down at her. "I'll expect an answer, Kendall— when you're ready. But for now, let's head back to the hotel. I think those kids wore you out."

Following as he led her carefully away from the cliff, Kendall asked blankly, "How did you know about the kids?" And saw him shrug.

"I called Father Thomas about an hour ago—on a hunch. He said you'd spent the day with the kids, and then headed this way."

Falling silent, Kendall glanced down at their clasped hands for a moment, then looked away. When would he ask his question again? And how would she answer?

C h a p t e r

4

Her new suite was a magnificent set of rooms on the top floor of the hotel, and Kendall could only wander a bit dazedly from room to room. She had left Hawke downstairs, since he'd been needed in the casino, and Rick had shown her to the suite.

At the moment Gypsy was sprawled across the king-size bed with a fine disregard for the lovely lace bedspread, and Kendall was staring, awed, at the beautiful oils adorning the pastel walls. It was undoubtedly a woman's suite. Ankle-deep carpet in pale gold, delicate Louis XIV furniture, floral wallpaper. The bath was huge, with a sunken tub, blue tiles, and gold fixtures. The sitting room contained a plush sofa and chairs, reading lamps.

Kendall had lived in houses with dirt floors and thatched roofs; this delicate grandeur was a bit unsettling.

But it was beautiful. So beautiful that she didn't notice the fly in the ointment for nearly an hour. The hotel staff had packed and unpacked for her, leaving her very little to do. Since it was nearly time for dinner, Kendall took a shower— saving the sunken tub for a more leisurely moment. She was wearing her robe and heading toward the closet when she suddenly noticed something different in the room.

Gypsy was peeking out from under the bed—a sure sign that she was disturbed. And on the bed was a tiny basket filled with assorted seashells and tied with a bright red ribbon.

It hadn't been there when she had gone in to take a shower.

Kendall was more than a little puzzled. The door was fastened from the inside with the night latch, the balcony doors also locked—from the inside. How could anyone have gotten into the room?

Thoughtfully, she examined the basket. It was not the sort of gift purchased in the hotel's gift shop. In fact, it took her only a moment to realize that someone had simply gone out on the beach and filled a decorative basket with shells. Shells? Someone?

Her glance moved slowly around the bedroom, then she stepped to the doorway and looked into the sitting room. And found it. One door too many. Logically, this door was just where it should be—if the suite connected with another one.

Still carrying the basket, Kendall crossed the room to the door and stared at it for a moment, then tried the knob. Unlocked. And no key on her side. Opening the door showed that there was no key on the other side either. But there was definitely another suite.

If her suite was a woman's, then this one was obviously a man's. No delicate furniture here, but massive, solid oak. The room was lived-in. Colorful pillows were piled on the carpeted floor in front of an extensive stereo system, magazines littered the coffee table, a huge oak desk stood in one corner by the balcony doors, covered with papers.

Moving slowly through the suite, Kendall found that the color scheme of deep brown and rust was continued in the bedroom. The bed was king-size, neatly made up. She halted by the dresser and gazed down at what was obviously a man's pocket change and wristwatch. Uh-huh. She knew that watch. Her life had taught her to be observant. And her earlier softened feelings toward the man hardened in a wave of anger. Damn him!

The sound of water splashing from the bathroom drew her attention, and Kendall headed in that direction, holding the basket in much the same way one would have hefted a hand grenade. She halted two steps into the room and stared at the deep brown sunken tub.

"I might have known." Her voice was a peculiar mixture of anger and resignation. "Do you *mind* telling me how I happened to land in the suite next door?"

"It was the only one available," Hawke replied innocently,

leaning back in the water and surveying her taut figure. "I'm sure Rick told you—"

"He told me. And—fool that I was—I believed him." Kendall kept her eyes fixed on his face, trying to ignore the expanse of hair-roughened, muscled chest visible from where she was standing. She held up the basket. "I presume you left this?"

"Of course." He languidly moved a large bath sponge across his chest, drawing her eyes in spite of herself. "A . . . memento of last night."

"I don't need any reminders, thank you!" she snapped. "What I *need* is another room."

"Sorry—none available. I don't see why you're so upset," he went on in a reasonable tone. "I've already given you my word not to force you into anything. And that suite's much nicer than the room you had before."

Quite suddenly Kendall's anger became directed at whoever had occupied that suite before her. A woman's room, and right next door to him . . . "I hope no one was—dispossessed—because of me," she said in a voice that sounded strange to her own ears.

Something very like satisfaction flickered in his gray eyes, and then was gone. "If you're inferring—and I gather you are —that the room was occupied by my—er—paramour, you couldn't be more wrong. It's usually reserved for my mother when she comes to visit."

Kendall didn't want to believe him. But she did.

"Would you like to wash my back?" he deadpanned, holding up the sponge.

"I'd like to drown you." She eyed him irritably.

He looked hurt. "At least thank me for the present."

Trying not to feel ungracious, Kendall shored up her dignity. "Thank you very much. But I can't possibly accept it, of course."

"Why not? I picked up some shells and put them in a basket, Kendall. It's not expensive, and certainly not what you could call an intimate present. Coming out!"

The warning gave Kendall scant time to turn her back, but she managed the feat. Face flaming, and cursing him silently for catching her off guard, she beat a hasty retreat back to her own rooms. And she was furious with herself.

Kendall was not easily embarrassed. She had been in parts of the world where naked bodies were the rule rather than the exception, and it had never bothered her. But this man had succeeded in embarrassing her more than she liked to remember. He kept her off guard and off balance . . . and unnerved.

She fought another cowardly impulse to run like a thief, placed the little basket with undue care on her nightstand, and began to get ready for dinner.

As Hawke had already noted, she had very few items in her wardrobe that *weren't* sexy. A weakness of hers—although not intended for seduction. Kendall just liked nice things. And since she rarely got the chance to wear them . . .

The dress was black. It was stark, unadorned by frills, and covered her from the neck to the ankles. That was, in front. The skirt was slit on one side almost to the waist, and her back was bare past the flare of her hips. It was impossible to wear anything under the dress, and the fact that she didn't was obvious.

Her sandals were also black, high-heeled, and difficult to walk in unless she was careful. Her only jewelry was a charm bracelet made of fine silver and filled with charms from all over the world. A small black clutch purse completed the outfit.

She checked Gypsy's food and water, sternly told the cat not to stray from the room (she was quite adept at opening unlocked doors), and then went into the sitting room. Almost immediately a cheerful knock sounded on the connecting door.

"Ready, Cinderella?" Hawke called through the door. "It's time we were off to the ball."

Composure intact, Kendall opened the door and stared at him. "Which of us turns into the frog at midnight?" she asked wryly.

"Neither of us." Resplendent in a black dinner jacket, Hawke placed a hand upon his chest and bowed mockingly. "My fairy godmother is lenient about such things. We have until dawn."

"And then?"

"And then we make our own magic."

Kendall sighed, trying to ignore the fact that her heart was beating alarmingly fast. "I hate to burst your bubble, but this is not a storybook romance."

"Want to bet?"

She stared into gray eyes shot with silver and felt the hard-won composure slipping. "Um—shouldn't we be going?" Hastily, she turned and started for the door of her suite, then heard a choked sound behind her. Looking over her shoulder, she found that Hawke was staring at her with a peculiar expression.

"My God," he muttered. "That thing's lethal!"

Kendall felt a short burst of triumph that she'd finally jarred *his* composure a bit, then realized that her revealing dress was somewhat comparable to waving a red flag at a bull. Not daring to respond to his statement, she preceded him quietly out into the hall, and watched while he closed and locked her door.

He led her down the hall to the elevator, his hand possessively cupping her elbow, and Kendall hastily squashed her momentary alarm. Surely he wouldn't try anything in the elevator again. Twice would be a habit, for God's sake!

Hawke was forming some very odd habits.

No sooner had the doors closed behind them than he drew her into his arms abruptly. Kendall had no chance to fend him off and, truth to tell, little strength to do so. Her traitorous body molded itself instantly to the hard length of his. But she did manage a moan of protest just before his lips covered hers.

And that, as the man said, was that. The protest was a small sop to her conscience, and left her body free to experience these delightful sensations.

His hands were hard and warm against her bare back, his lips demanding—and receiving—a response. Mindlessly, Kendall felt his tongue probing the sensitive inner surface of her lips, and a shiver of helpless desire coursed through her body. She felt one of his hands move around and begin to creep up her rib cage, and then there was a quiet swish, and someone cleared his throat.

Vaguely disappointed that his hand had not reached its destination, Kendall opened her eyes slowly to watch his head moving back. Sanity returned in a rush as he released her, and she glanced at the elevator doors to see two men smiling at her apologetically.

Heedless of the listeners, she snapped at Hawke, "Dammit! If you do this to me again . . . !"

"Temper, temper." He grinned at her, apparently undisturbed by the embrace. But Kendall could see his eyes only just losing their glazed appearance, and knew that he wasn't quite as indifferent as he seemed.

Dutch comfort.

Vastly angry at the world in general, and the male half in

particular, she stalked from the elevator, gritting her teeth silently when Hawke joined her and smoothly took her elbow.

Of course, she couldn't stay angry at him. At last night's cozy table for two, he kept up a steady stream of casual, amusing conversation, surprising a giggle out of her on more than one occasion. She found herself relaxing, enjoying the meal and him.

After dinner he took her into a large room she'd never seen before, a combination bar and dance floor. It was moderately crowded, but he had no trouble in securing a small, private booth for them.

He had called out an order to the bartender as they passed, and Kendall looked suspiciously at the peculiar-looking drink placed in front of her moments later. It resembled a pineapple filled with a harmless-looking liquid and decorated with assorted fruit slices, an umbrella, and a straw. "What *is* this?"

He sat back, sipping his brandy, then answered casually, "It's called a Purple Passion."

She stared at him for a moment, then looked down at the drink. "It doesn't look the least bit purple," she said, straight-faced.

"Sorry."

"What's in it?"

"Fruit punch. Orange juice, grape juice, pineapple juice—and so on. Live a little," he advised, smiling slowly.

Kendall took a cautious sip. Then a larger one. "Not bad." It was good, in fact. And very relaxing. Within minutes, everything Hawke said to her became terribly amusing.

When he asked her to dance about half an hour later, the drink was nearly gone and Kendall stumbled slightly in leaving the booth. It didn't concern her. The high-heeled sandals had always been hell to walk in.

Kendall had never in her life been drunk. It was partly a matter of innate horror at the thought of losing control of herself, and partly a dislike for the taste of alcohol. In any case, she had never been even the slightest bit tipsy. So she didn't recognize the signs.

On the dance floor she went into Hawke's arms, her own arms slipping up around his neck instinctively. She was mildly dismayed by her desire to cling to him, but then her attention became caught by a very funny-looking man who was a member of the small band playing busily in the corner, and she giggled and forgot the dismay.

"You dance very well," Hawke murmured softly.

Kendall rested her cheek against his chest and wondered dreamily why her feet weren't touching the floor. "That's what the sheikh said," she responded vaguely.

"Sheikh?"

"Ummm. He wanted me to be number-three wife. But I told him that I couldn't play second fiddle . . . much less third fiddle." She lifted her head and stared up at Hawke with a frown. "I can't play the fiddle at all."

"And what did the sheikh say?" Hawke prompted, seemingly amused.

"He tried to buy me from Daddy." She frowned again. "Daddy was terribly rude, I'm afraid."

"I can imagine." He pulled her a bit closer to avoid another couple dancing enthusiastically past.

Kendall clung to him happily.

Somehow, they made it through the dance, and Hawke led her back to their booth. Kendall practically fell onto the leather-covered seat, giggling softly, and watched Hawke slide in across from her.

"Kendall . . ." He hesitated, then went on dryly. "You don't drink very much, do you?"

"Oh, I don't drink at all," she told him sunnily. "I can't stand the taste." She discovered, to her disappointment, that the Purple Passion was gone, and pushed the pineapple-glass across the table to Hawke. "May I have another of these, please?"

He stared at her, then looked up and signaled the bartender. "Of course," he murmured in a peculiar voice.

Sometime later—Kendall wasn't particularly concerned with the time—Hawke came around to drop her purse in her lap and then swing her up into his arms. Somehow. Kendall was impressed with the feat, but a little puzzled.

Linking her fingers together at the back of his neck, she asked mildly, "Why are you carrying me? You always carry me."

"Romance," he said, carrying her through the interested crowd in the bar.

Kendall didn't return the crowd's interest; hers was focused entirely on Hawke's face. She nodded wisely. "Storybook romance."

"That's right. Although I have to admit, honey—you couldn't make it up to your room alone. Not tonight."

"Am I drunk?" she asked curiously.

"Slightly."

"Oh. I don't feel drunk." Thinking about that, Kendall was slightly surprised to find that they had reached the elevator. This time the ride up was shared with an older woman whose face Kendall recognized vaguely but couldn't put a name to.

Pushing the problem aside, she smiled brightly at the woman. "Hi. I'm Kendall. And this is Hawke." She unlinked her fingers long enough to pat Hawke on the top of his head.

"Hi." The woman's lips twitched strangely. "I'm Amanda." She glanced at Hawke and added severely, "Shame on you!"

Kendall felt Hawke's shoulder shaking with silent laughter, and realized that Amanda had said something funny. She didn't know what it was, but she smiled anyway.

Amanda got off the elevator, apparently on her floor, and

then Hawke and Kendall rode the rest of the way to the top floor alone. By the time they reached the door to Kendall's suite, she was staring in utter fascination at Hawke's face. It seemed, oddly, that she had never really looked at him before.

Halting in front of Kendall's door, he met her intense gaze and seemed to have trouble speaking. His voice sounded hoarse. "I don't suppose you can get your key out."

Abruptly, the intensity melted from Kendall's expression. "I couldn't find an elephant if it poked me with its trunk," she told him solemnly, then dissolved into giggles.

Sighing, Hawke set her carefully on her feet, grabbing the purse before it could drop to the floor. He had to lean Kendall against the doorjamb while he unlocked the door, and even then she showed a tendency to slide toward the floor. She was still giggling.

The door opened at last, Hawke picked her up again and strode inside, kicking it shut behind them. He carried her through the sitting room, and Kendall only dimly noticed Gypsy curled up on the sofa. She became aware of her surroundings only when Hawke set her carefully on the bed and turned on a lamp on the nightstand.

He stared down at her for a moment, then said roughly, "I know damn well you can't get undressed by yourself. The thing is—I *don't* know if I can undress you and then leave."

Quite sanely, Kendall realized that she wanted him to stay

with her. Always. Forever. Artlessly, she held out her arms to him. "You don't have to leave."

"Kendall—"

"Please don't leave." Her eyes filled with tears. "I don't like to be alone in the dark, Hawke. Stay with me. . . ."

He groaned softly, abruptly reaching to pull her up from the bed and into his arms. Kendall could feel his fingers at the back of her neck, unfastening the single clasp that held up her dress, even as his mouth took hers with hungry intensity.

Not even in the back of her mind was there a token protest. She wanted him desperately, her slender body flaming with a desire so powerful that it felt as if it scorched her. Her trembling fingers pushed the jacket from his shoulders, and she felt her dress slide to the floor with only a whisper of sound.

Hawke raised his head to look down at her, silver flames in his eyes. "You're so beautiful," he whispered raggedly, his gaze devouring her body.

Kendall felt herself lifted, and then she was aware of the softness of the bed beneath her back. Dimly, she realized that the maid must have turned down the covers, but it was only a fleeting thought. She lay silently and watched with dazed eyes as Hawke impatiently removed his clothes.

When he came down on the bed beside her, Kendall again held out her arms to him, and his eyes flared oddly as he accepted the silent invitation. He covered her face and throat with gentle, passionate kisses, his hands exploring her body with growing urgency.

Kendall moaned softly when one hand cupped a swelling breast, her breath catching in her throat. She had never known such feelings were possible, fire licking along her veins as his mouth captured a throbbing nipple. She wanted him to stop what he was doing, to never stop. She locked her fingers in his thick hair, her body straining instinctively against him.

Hawke muttered something she didn't hear, his mouth concentrating on first one nipple and then the other, his hands moving over her flesh with sensual abrasiveness.

She slid her hands over his back wonderingly, feeling muscles tense beneath her fingers. He was so strong, she thought dimly. So strong. Strong enough to take care of her.

Odd. Where had that thought come from?

He lifted his head suddenly with a soft laugh and reached for her left wrist. Fumbling with the clasp of her charm bracelet, he whispered teasingly, "It's scratching me!"

It was the wrong thing to say; for some reason the statement struck Kendall as being exquisitely funny. And, once started, the giggles just wouldn't stop.

Giggling helplessly, Kendall didn't realize at first that Hawke was no longer making love to her. When she finally managed some measure of control, she found that he was raised on an elbow beside her, his expression resigned.

A small, reasonably sober portion of her brain told her

that this wasn't working out quite the way Hawke had planned. She had a feeling that this particular type of laughter didn't exactly stoke the fires of passion. Her own desire had faded anyway.

"I—I'm sorry," she gasped at last, choking off a final giggle. "I don't know what's wrong with me."

"I do." He sighed and regretfully drew the covers up over their naked bodies. "But it's probably better this way. You would have hated yourself in the morning. And gone after *me* with a knife!"

She was mildly shocked. "I wouldn't do that."

"Of course not."

"I'm not a shrew."

"No." He smiled suddenly and traced a gentle finger down her nose. "Right now, you're a little girl."

Kendall didn't understand what was happening. Not then. She knew only that something inside her began to throb with an awful pain at his words. Hot tears filled her throat and threatened to flood the locked room in her mind. She didn't want to face that hurting memory. She didn't want to. . . .

"Kendall?" Hawke placed an arm across her, gazing down at her with worried eyes. "Honey, what's wrong?"

"Little girl." Her whisper was filled with pain. "Oh, Hawke, she was such a beautiful little girl! So sweet. With a smile like sunshine."

"Who, honey?" he asked gently. "Who are you talking about?"

"Rosita . . . little rose . . ."

His arm tightened across her waist. In a soft, intense voice, he told her, "You have to talk about it, Kendall. It's eating you up inside. Tell me!"

"It was—in South America." She was vaguely surprised that her voice was steady, the tears still held at bay. She was even more surprised that she was telling him something that had haunted her for months. Not even her father knew the whole story.

"Tell me, honey."

"She was an orphan. I played with the kids every day, and when I saw Rosita—I fell in love with her. She used to gather wildflowers to give me every day. And we'd go for long walks and watch butterflies. I loved her so *much,* Hawke!" She stared up at him, choking back a dry sob.

"What happened?" he asked quietly, smoothing back a strand of hair from her forehead.

Kendall swallowed hard. "The revolution started," she told him with painful control. "I went to help evacuate the orphans—there were nearly fifty of them in that tiny place, and the Sisters needed help. The revolutionaries didn't care who got hurt; they didn't care about innocent children. We had to take them somewhere safe.

"We were leading them along the road and Rosita—broke

away from the others. I tried to reach her, but I wasn't fast enough. And I couldn't leave the other children. I called out to her, but she'd seen some flowers in a field, and ran toward them."

"And then?" Hawke's voice was tight.

"She looked over her shoulder at me, laughing." Kendall's voice was toneless. "And . . . tripped a mine."

With a soft groan Hawke gathered her in his arms and held her tightly. "God, I'm sorry, honey! I'm so sorry."

"I couldn't cry for her, Hawke," Kendall went on in the same toneless, suspended voice. "I had to get the other children away from there. And I couldn't even stop to cry for her. I wanted to go back later . . . but they wouldn't let me."

"Honey—"

"She died because of me . . . and those damned flowers. And I've never been able to cry for her."

"Kendall, it wasn't your fault," he told her firmly, one hand gently stroking her soft hair. "You couldn't have stopped it."

She rolled away from him suddenly on the wide bed, turning her back to him and drawing the covers up around her neck with a shiver. Dimly, she understood that he couldn't be allowed to comfort her—not about this. His gentle understanding was tapping the well of tears deep inside of her. And, she very much feared, if the tears once started, they might never stop.

Something small and stubborn within her refused to cry for Rosita. To cry would be to admit that she was gone. Even the pain would be gone, and there would be only an aching emptiness. It was the emptiness Kendall was afraid of. She would be alone in the emptiness with nothing to hold on to.

"Kendall . . ." Hawke firmly grasped her shoulder and pulled her over onto her back, staring down at her tense face. His own face was strangely vulnerable. "Share your pain with me, honey. Let me hold you. I know how you feel." His voice roughened. "I know."

She stared up at him for a moment, and then her eyes dropped to a small mark high on his chest. Near the left shoulder, it was almost unnoticeable because of his deep tan. Her fingers reached to touch the small scar, and she remembered Father Thomas telling her that Hawke had been wounded while evacuating children from a small hospital. Kendall had seen too many bullet wounds not to recognize one when she saw it.

He knew. Something inside her crumbled, and she buried her face in his throat, hot tears releasing her grief after months of rigid self-control.

Hawke held her close, murmuring soothingly but making no attempt to halt her tears. He simply shared the warmth of his body, the comforting touch of another human being.

Afterward, Kendall was totally drained, and more weary than she had ever been. She was lying with her head on

Hawke's shoulder, only dimly aware of their naked bodies pressed close together. She felt him shift slightly, and the light on the nightstand went out.

"I couldn't save her, Hawke."

"I know."

"But I should have been able to save her. If I'd done something differently—"

"It wouldn't have made a difference." His voice was very quiet. "Stop torturing yourself, honey. Just believe that she's at peace now. No one can hurt her again."

"It's so hard. To see her die that way . . ."

"Remember the good times." His voice was soothing, almost hypnotic. "Remember her that way."

Kendall felt an unfamiliar peace steal over her, and she snuggled closer to his hard body. A faint realization formed in her mind, but she was too tired to be angry by it. "Hawke?"

"What is it, darling?"

The new endearment warmed her oddly. "You deliberately got me drunk, didn't you?" When he remained silent, she persisted sleepily. "You did, didn't you?"

He sighed softly. "Not exactly. I just didn't discourage you from drinking when I realized you weren't used to it."

"Sneaky."

"Always."

Kendall yawned. "Why can't I get angry with you?"

"You'll be angry with me," he answered whimsically. "In the morning."

She was too sleepy to understand the remark. Her thoughts faded away into nothingness and she slept.

The dreams were confused at first. Princesses sleeping on impossibly high beds, dragons and witches and spells. She could hear children laughing, but couldn't see them. She walked through a wooded area, puzzled by the seashells on the path and the armored knight who kept charging past her on a white horse.

She bowed gravely to a wizard throwing stardust into the air and chanting a spell, then stepped carefully around the small audience of solemnly watching elves. Moments later she passed a tea party going on beneath a huge tree. There was another elf, something that might have been a troll, the armored knight—and his horse—and an economy-size dragon toasting marshmallows. The dragon offered Kendall a marshmallow; she declined politely and walked on.

The children's laughter was growing louder, and she headed toward the sound. There was a vague urgency driving her; she had to find the children. But the path seemed to wind on forever. She passed a tower with a rope made of hair dangling from the single window. She passed a puzzled prince trying vainly to fit the glass slipper he carried onto a buxom maid's foot. She passed a castle with banners flying.

She passed a little boy trying to jump over a candlestick,

and thought irritably, *That's not right—this is supposed to be a fairy tale, not a nursery rhyme!*

Another knight rode by—this one in black armor and riding a black horse—and she rather uncertainly curtsied as he bowed to her. Odd. Weren't the black knights supposed to be the bad guys?

Her thoughts were distracted as she realized that she was wearing a beautiful gown, fit for any princess. Holding the pure white skirt up carefully, she walked on.

As she emerged from the woods at last, she found herself in a rolling meadow with wildflowers growing everywhere. A group of children were playing happily, laughing and chasing one another.

Smiling, Kendall hurried toward them, her gaze fixed on a little black-haired girl with huge brown eyes.

And then a dark cloud blotted out the sun, and Kendall broke into a run, desperate to reach the little girl. She heard the black knight thundering toward her, shouting a warning. And then an explosion rent the air. Kendall stopped running and stared down at her once-white dress, stained terribly now. The knight was swearing roughly, and all the children were staring at her with fear and horror in their eyes. All but one . . .

Her own scream woke Kendall from the nightmare, and she found herself struggling in Hawke's arms as he tried to calm her. The struggles ceased immediately and she clung to him, hearing the soft, swearing voice of the black knight in her dream.

"It's all right, honey—you're safe now," he murmured.

"Hawke—it happened again," she sobbed painfully. "It happened again in the dream. Make it stop . . . please make it stop!"

He soothed her gently with his voice and his hands and, after a time, she became calm again. She was only barely aware when he pulled the covers back up around them.

"Stay with me," she whispered, already half-asleep.

"I will," he told her softly.

Kendall thought that he'd said something else, but she was drifting back into a pleasant dream, and the words disturbed and puzzled her.

Why would the black knight say that he loved her . . . ?

C h a p t e r

An ungodly racket woke Kendall late the next morning, and she winced in pain as she half fell out of the bed. At least a dozen elves seemed to have taken up residence in her head, and they were building something with huge hammers.

And the pounding that was presently coming from the door of her suite wasn't helping matters.

Kendall was halfway to the bedroom door before she realized that she wasn't wearing a stitch of clothing. Holding her throbbing head with one hand, she managed to locate the closet and her robe. She even managed to put it on. Then she stalked—carefully—to the door of the suite, flung it open, and snapped, *"What?"*

Immediately, the sound of her own voice echoed cruelly in her head, and she clutched it with both hands, staring with bleary eyes at her inconsiderate visitor.

It was Rick. A somewhat hesitant Rick, staring at her and holding a black sandal in one hand.

Kendall returned the stare and wished that something in this situation made sense. Try as she would, the night before was a complete blank. Except for that damned Purple Passion.

"Miss James?" he asked hesitantly, as if there were some doubt. "I came to return this." He handed her the shoe.

Kendall stared at *it* for a moment, accepted it, then looked back at Rick.

"There's a message," he offered solemnly, his lips twitching.

"Please," Kendall whispered, "not so loud. What's the message?"

"Quote: 'Tell Cinderella that she must have lost her slipper in the lobby. She should be more careful.' Unquote."

"Coward. Why couldn't he deliver the message himself?"

Rick shrugged. "He had to go to the other hotel for a while. Said it'd be safer if he stayed out of range today." The manager appeared to have a hard time keeping a straight face. "I see you're—uh—a little under the weather, Miss James."

"Under the weather?" Kendall would have laughed hysterically if she'd thought her head could take it. "I'd have to feel better to die." Before he could do more than grin sympathetically, she went on flatly. "Would you deliver a message for me, Mr. Evans?"

"Rick. And sure I will."

She nodded and winced again. "I want you to repeat exactly what I tell you to your conveniently absent boss and the bartender downstairs."

"Okay."

"Quote: 'Cinderella knows a hundred and three ways to cause acute pain to the parts of your body you prize the most. And just as soon as her head decides to stay on, she's going to practice a hundred and two of those methods on you.' Unquote. Got it?"

"Got it." Rick was definitely trying not to laugh. "Would you like for me to send up some aspirin, Miss James?"

"Kendall," she corrected him automatically. "No, thank you. I have some with me."

"I would suggest breakfast, but—"

The hand holding Kendall's head slipped down to cover her mouth, and she gave him a painfully goaded look. "No," she mumbled around her fingers, "please don't make that suggestion."

"Sorry." He backed away rather hastily. "If you need anything, just call—"

"I know. Room service." She closed the door carefully.

For the next hour or so, Kendall didn't think. She swallowed a couple of aspirin, hung out the Do Not Disturb sign on her door, and then filled the sunken tub in her bathroom with steaming water. Then she soaked. For at least an hour.

Emerging at last from the bath, she felt reasonably human

—given another million or so years of evolution, that is. Automatically, she put on her black bikini, thinking vaguely that perhaps the sun would bake the remaining poisons out of her system. Then she pulled on a pair of shorts and a T-shirt.

She was just coming out of her bedroom, when she noticed two things. Gypsy's entrance into the room from Hawke's suite distracted her attention from the other thing. She walked across the room and closed the door firmly behind the big cat.

"So that's where you were. Defected to the enemy camp, I see." Gypsy ignored the stern voice, leaping up onto the sofa and beginning to wash a forepaw.

Kendall sighed, and then turned to contemplate the other thing. It was sitting on the small desk by the door, and it was just lovely. A Paul Revere bowl, made of gleaming copper and holding a leafy green plant. She didn't immediately recognize the plant.

It hadn't been there the night before. She was sure of it. Well, almost sure of it. Had Hawke put it there? She approached the bowl warily and stared at it. A moment's study convinced her that Hawke had sent it. There was a tiny bird stamped delicately into the copper near the lip of the bowl. A hawk, she was sure.

Muttering to herself, she reached out a hand to touch the plant, then drew back abruptly as she recognized the plant. "You're a Venus's-flytrap," she told the plant in a bemused voice. "Why would he give me a Venus's-flytrap?"

It was at that point that she realized the night before deserved some serious thought. She went over to sit on the sofa beside Gypsy, absently scratching the cat beneath her chin.

She remembered the drink. And the dancing. And she remembered laughing quite a lot. Too much, in fact. The longer she sat and thought, the more she remembered.

A merciful God would have left the evening a total blank.

Kendall was glad there was no one present as she slowly relived the night before. She had asked him—no, dammit, *begged* him—to stay with her, she remembered. And he had. She could remember everything else. What she had done, what she had said . . .

Surprised, she realized that she could think of Rosita now without that dreadful pain. Hawke had been right—sharing the pain had eased it. She would always be grateful to him for that.

But the rest . . .

She decided to be angry about the rest. It would be safer that way. If nothing else, the anger would sharpen her survival instincts. She needed that small edge. Never mind everything they had in common. Never mind the fact that he had seen a side of her she'd never shown anyone else. Never mind.

She wouldn't let herself love him.

Love was dangerous. It was reckless, foolish, and potentially painful. No matter what tricks Hawke pulled out of his hat, she wouldn't give in to him. She wouldn't let him go to her head, or her heart; she wouldn't become his summer fling.

And she damn sure wouldn't drink another Purple Passion.

Having made those firm decisions, Kendall gathered up her beachbag, dropped her room keys inside, and headed out. She didn't warn Gypsy to stay in the room. *Let* her sharpen her claws on Hawke's sofa. It would teach him not to send Venus's-flytraps to puzzled women.

She found Rick in the lobby by the desk, and something he'd said to her earlier tugged at Kendall's mind.

"You're looking better," he greeted her cheerfully.

"Beast. Never tell a woman she's looking better; it makes you sound very ungentlemanly." Taking pity on his bemusement, she waved away the comment and asked curiously, "Did you say Hawke was at the other hotel?"

He nodded. "That's right. A problem with the staff that he had to deal with."

"He owns the other hotel on the island?"

"Sure."

Kendall propped an elbow on the desk and stared at him. She should have known. She really should have. "Tell me," she said carefully, "does this island have a name?"

"Of course." Rick sounded surprised that she didn't know. "It's called Isle of the Hawk."

She leaned her forehead on a raised hand and sighed softly. "Don't tell me. He owns the whole damn island?"

Rick's smile held a trace of sympathetic amusement.

" 'Fraid so. It's been in the family for generations. A buc-
caneering ancestor—Hawke's namesake—used this island as a
base of operations way back when pirates roamed the seas. The
island got its name from him."

Kendall frowned slightly. "Hawke told me that he bought
the hotel."

"He did. After 'Nam, he traveled for a while. Kept coming
back to this place. When his father died, he traded some of his
family stock for the island—and the hotels. He has two younger
brothers who manage the family holdings in the States." Rick
shrugged. "Then he called me in to manage for him."

Several things fell into place in Kendall's mind. "You were
with him in Vietnam. You're the 'mutual friend' Father Thomas
was talking about."

Rick looked blank for a moment, then nodded with a faint
smile. "I'm the one who talked to Father Thomas about
Hawke, if that's what you mean. And we were in 'Nam together
—in the same squad."

"And the tattoo?" she asked wryly.

"Tattoo?" He seemed startled, but then comprehension
came and he grinned. "Oh—the hawk. Yes, I'm one of the guys
responsible for that. We had fun that night," he added reminis-
cently.

"I'm sure." Kendall started to say more, but her attention
was caught by an older woman who was passing the desk and

smiling at her. The woman from the elevator last night? Amanda?

"Feeling better?" the woman asked Kendall cheerfully.

"Oh . . . fine, thank you," Kendall managed to answer weakly. She watched until the woman had left the lobby, then looked at Rick. Obviously, he was trying to stifle laughter. "I suppose you think something's funny?" she muttered irritably.

"Funnier than you know." Rick made an effort to straighten his face. "That lady was Mrs. Foster. This morning she extended her reservation another week. She told me that she just had to see how the romance turned out."

Kendall didn't believe him. It was absurd, of course. She glared at him. "You just wait!" Her voice was threatening. "One of these days, you'll get yours—and I hope I'm around to see it. I'll laugh myself silly!"

"You'll be around," he said with a peculiar smile. "If it ever happens."

"It will." She ignored the first part of his statement, turning on her heel and stalking toward the doors leading out to the pool. She could hear him laughing behind her, and the sound set the seal on her temper.

She passed the pool without a glance, intent on finding one of the shaded lounges she'd seen on the beach. The path was deserted, the beach nearly so. Most of the hotel guests, she decided, were having lunch. Kendall wasn't hungry.

She shed her shorts and T-shirt, fished in her beachbag for

her sunglasses and a paperback novel, then settled down on the shaded lounge she had chosen.

A few minutes later a young waiter came out and placed a small table by the lounge. On the table he set a frosty glass. Kendall stared at it. "What's this?"

"Mr. Evans sent it out, Miss James."

She took a sip of the fruity drink, then looked suspiciously at the young man. "What's in it?"

He looked bewildered. "Fruit juice, Miss James."

Kendall didn't like the looks of the tiny umbrella jutting out of the glass. "That had better be all that's in it," she told the young man ominously.

Nodding hesitantly, he beat a hasty retreat, still looking bewildered.

Kendall felt a giggle pushing its way up, and sternly repressed it. Determined, she went back to her novel. Hopefully, it would discourage casual conversation from anyone walking by. It did.

Hours later she was nearing the end of the book, and the sun was beginning to sink in the western sky. She had gotten up a couple of times to reposition the umbrella shading her, but other than that, she hadn't moved all afternoon.

She glanced up absently, and barely managed to keep from jumping when she saw Hawke standing at the foot of the lounge and staring at her. He was wearing slacks and a knit shirt, and looked as if he weren't quite sure what her reaction would be. Kendall wasn't sure either.

"I got your message," he offered finally.

"Good. Take it to heart."

He sighed, and assumed a ridiculously woeful expression. "Have a little pity for me. There I was, all set to have the night of my life—and the lady in my arms kept being attacked by fits of the giggles." His voice was pained.

Kendall silently held up one hand, thumb and forefinger rubbing gently together.

Hawke stared at the gesture. "What's that?"

"This," Kendall told him succinctly, "is the smallest violin in the world, playing hearts and flowers just for you." Halting the gesture, she turned her attention back to her book.

"Well, thanks." His voice held a tremor of laughter. "No sympathy from you, I see."

"None." She was grateful for the shielding sunglasses, which were hiding the gleam of laughter in her eyes.

"My little gift of apology didn't help, obviously."

"Why a Venus's-flytrap?" Kendall felt irritated at her curiosity, and added with great dignity, "Not that I can accept it."

"You'll hurt my feelings if you don't." He sat down on the end of the lounge, regarding her thoughtfully. "And I picked that because it reminded me of you."

She waited a beat, then asked carefully, "I remind you of a carnivorous plant?"

"Sure." Hawke smiled slowly. "Beautiful, deceptively fragile, and potentially deadly."

Kendall started to say that she'd been compared to worse things, then realized that she *hadn't*. "Thanks."

"You're welcome," he responded solemnly.

She decided that if *he* wasn't going to mention last night's confession, *she* certainly wasn't. It probably hadn't meant anything to him anyway. In spite of what she'd thought. "I'm trying to read this book, you know," she pointed out.

"Sorry." He got to his feet. "I just came to say good-bye."

"You—you're leaving?" It was the last thing she had expected.

The response seemed to satisfy him. "For a couple of days. I have some business in Florida. Will you miss me?"

"Dreadfully!" she snapped, angry at herself for the betraying uncertainty. "How soon are you leaving?"

"Right away." He was amused now. "Helicopter to Nassau, then a plane to Miami."

"Have a nice trip." Resolutely, she went back to the book.

"Not so fast." He reached down to grip her upper arms firmly, pulling her effortlessly to her feet. "Not without a kiss good-bye."

"Hawke!" she protested as he removed her sunglasses and tossed them onto the lounge. "I can't—I won't—dammit, stop manhandling me!"

He took the book away from her and tossed it on the

lounge. "A kiss for luck," he told her reproachfully. "It's a savage world out there. Never know what I might run into. Isn't a maiden supposed to give her knight a kiss for luck?"

"No," Kendall said a little desperately. "She gives him a scarf to wear into battle. But since you're *not* my knight, you're *not* going into battle, and I *don't* happen to have a scarf handy, it doesn't really matter!"

"A kiss will do."

She stared up at him for a moment, then muttered "Oh, hell." And she swayed toward him, her face lifted invitingly.

There was a slight pause, and then Hawke kissed her. On the forehead. Chastely. Just like a knight in the age of chivalry. If Kendall had been holding something heavy, she would have hit him with it.

"Bye, honey." His deep voice was threaded with laughter.

Kendall sank down on the lounge as he released her arms, not trusting herself to speak. And it didn't help her temper one bit to see that several hotel guests had watched the little scene with great interest.

Hawke started to turn away, then looked back at her as though he'd had a sudden thought. "What would you like me to bring you from Florida?" he asked cheerfully.

She picked up her sunglasses from the lounge and shoved them onto her nose. "That," she told him carefully, "is a dangerous question to ask me right now."

"Oh." His lips twitched slightly. "Sorry. I'll just find something on my own; how's that?"

"Don't go to any trouble on my account," she advised him politely.

Grinning, he started toward the hotel, throwing one last remark over his shoulder. "Don't forget me, now!"

"Fat chance," Kendall muttered to herself. Resolutely, she picked up her novel again and began to read. Half an hour later, still reading the same page, she swore softly and dropped the novel into her beachbag. And she didn't even feel a twinge of dismay when she realized that the book had completely lost its appeal.

She rose from the lounge, pulled on her shorts and T-shirt, and headed for the hotel, swinging the beachbag as though she wanted to throw it at someone. Unfortunately, the target she was longing for had already left.

There was a package waiting for her at the desk. It was about five inches square, three inches deep, and wrapped in glittering silver paper. And there was a small card tucked into a snowy envelope. Kendall didn't say a word as she accepted the package from Rick. She even resisted an impulse to tear into the envelope when she was alone in the elevator.

Common sense told her it was from Hawke. Temper told her to drop it from her balcony. Dignity and pride commanded her to place the gift in his suite—unopened. Curiosity ate at her.

Alone in her suite, Kendall dropped her beachbag, sank on to the sofa, and hastily opened the envelope. *This is your symbol,* he'd written on the card, the handwriting as bold and decisive as the man himself. *A creature of myth and legend, lovely and fragile . . . and just slightly unreal. Hawke.*

Kendall was almost afraid to open the box. But she did. And a soft "Oh!" escaped her as she carefully lifted the delicate cut-glass unicorn from the tissue paper. It was absolutely beautiful.

She wanted to cry. Half angrily, she realized that there always seemed to be a cloudburst just over the horizon these days. Oh, God, what was the man *doing* to her? He made her laugh, made her angry, made her cry. In two short days he'd literally turned her life upside down.

Never in her life had she known a man like him. When most men wooed a woman, they sent flowers, candy, perfume. Not Hawke. He sent seashells. And carnivorous plants in expensive copper bowls. And unicorns. What had he told her? That knowing him would be an education? Damn the man— right again.

Kendall cradled the glass creature in her hands and stared down at it. Beautiful things such as this were her weakness, but she had never gotten the chance to collect them. Living as she did, out of suitcases, it just wasn't practical. Had he guessed?

She wondered vaguely if he had written the note with a straight face. And knew that he had. He was a strange man,

Hawke Madison. She had already noticed that his staff treated him with the utmost respect. Instinct told her that he would be formidable indeed if he were roused to temper. He'd come of age in a brutal war and, God knew, that would harden a man.

And yet . . . the sensitivity was there. He loved children. He could cheerfully sweep a woman off her feet and carry her through a crowded lobby or bar. He could talk of fairy tales and myths. He could hold her gently in his arms as she cried, sharing the pain of grief and a nightmare.

A romantic man. A *storybook* romantic man. And what woman could resist that?

Kendall wasn't angry with him any longer—if, indeed, she had ever been angry in the first place. And that was a bad sign. A very bad sign.

Rick escorted her to dinner that night—something that Kendall didn't question until they were at their table. She found Rick to be uncomplicated next to his friend and employer, and had no trouble at all in talking to him. The conversation flowed easily between them.

Kendall's question was calm, but she timed it so that Rick was somewhat involved with eating. "Did Hawke tell you to do this?"

Her escort choked and hastily reached for his wineglass,

then looked at her with watering, faintly accusing eyes. "Of course not," he said stoutly.

He was a bad liar.

She sighed and went on with her meal, not even able to conjure up a flash of temper. And her involuntary thought of *Damn the man!* was more rueful than anything else. Her thoughts were distracted, though, when Rick began to speak.

"You know, you're not at all what I thought you were," he commented slowly, watching her. "When you came in the other day, I thought you were—well—" He made a vague gesture.

"The phrase," Kendall told him dryly, "is 'dumb blonde.' A little game I used to play."

"Did you enjoy the game?" His brown eyes gleamed cheerfully.

"Immensely. I never had to carry my own luggage."

"Then why did you stop?" Rick smiled faintly. "Hawke?"

Staring down at the fork in her hand, Kendall only then noticed that it was monogramed. Stamped into the silver was a tiny bird. It might have been an eagle. Or even a particularly handsome chicken. Except that it was a hawk. It was very discreet; she never would have noticed it except that the subject tended to prey on her mind.

Looking up at Rick, she gave a shrug and asked in a defeated tone, "Can we please talk about something else?"

Trying unsuccessfully to hide his grin, Rick obligingly changed the subject.

On Wings of Magic

The next two days were a somewhat trying test of Kendall's composure. Hawke might not have been present in the flesh, but his spirit was slowly boxing her in. Reminders of him were everywhere. Hotel stationery stamped with a tiny hawk. The tennis racket she used to play tennis with Rick—again, stamped with a hawk. Small emblems on the clothing of the hotel staff.

Escaping from the hotel on the second day, Kendall went to the orphanage and played with the children for a while, then walked back through the village. Stopping before the window of a gift shop, she stared wryly at two figurines of hawks. The first was a somewhat savage hawk clasping a thankfully unidentified victim in his talons. The second—shaking Kendall oddly—was a more sensitive scene. Two hawks hovering over a nest filled with their young.

Turning hastily away, she came face-to-face with a sign hanging over the doorway of a nearby building. The Hawk's Nest Tavern.

It was enough to drive a woman crazy.

And then there were the gifts. They were always waiting for her at the desk—although there were no more notes. On the first day there was one delivered to her by Rick as she was passing the desk on her way back from breakfast. It was a stained-glass suncatcher, complete with a fine chain to hang it in a window. The workmanship was exquisite, and the scene was a rainbow—complete with a pot of gold. There was a tiny bird on the pot.

On the second day there was another suncatcher—this time with a unicorn beneath the rainbow and prancing toward the pot of gold. After dinner she was given another silver-wrapped box. This one held a small brass paperweight bearing another unicorn.

By the morning of the third day Kendall was wishing desperately for Hawke to come back just so she could strangle him. It wasn't that she was angry. It would have been *impossible* to be angered by such wonderfully romantic gifts.

Still, she wanted to strangle him. He'd begun this absurd courtship beneath the eyes of a hotel full of strangers, and everyone was interested in the outcome. And they were no longer strangers. She'd been approached by all of them at one time or another. Some just said hello, others told her soothingly that Mr. Madison would soon return. The men were a bit wary —apparently considering her staked out as private property— and the women were openly envious.

Some, like Amanda Foster, offered advice on how to tether a hawk. Others merely smiled in an unusually friendly manner. It was like living in a very small town.

So Kendall was feeling a bit desperate as she approached the desk in the lobby early on the third morning. With a calm expression belied by the frantic gleam in her blue-green eyes, she leaned against the desk and looked steadily at Rick.

He reached beneath the desk and pulled out another package.

Kendall propped both elbows on the desk and covered her face with her hands. "What's he trying to do to me?" she moaned.

"I think you know!" Rick was openly laughing.

She gave him a goaded stare and tore into the package. It was a set of delicate wind chimes, made of seashells. Kendall stared at them for a moment, then carefully put them back into the box. "How did he know I loved wind chimes?" she asked herself.

Rick took it upon himself to offer an answer. "Maybe he reads minds."

"Oh, God. That *would* be the final straw." Gathering up her package, Kendall started to turn away, then hesitated. "I think I'll have breakfast in my room. Rick, could you send up a very small bowl of ground hamburger?"

"For breakfast?" He looked startled.

"No. I'll call room service for my breakfast."

"Oh. For Gypsy?" Like the rest of the staff, Rick had become fairly well acquainted with Kendall's feline pet.

Kendall sighed. "No. For my plant. There are very few flies in this hotel." She headed for the elevator, not noticing the puzzled stare that followed her.

She fed her plant, her cat, and herself, then set the plant on the balcony for sun and took Gypsy for a walk on the beach.

The rest of the day was spent in her suite, where she spent a great deal of time staring at Hawke's presents.

And she had an awful feeling that she was going down for the third time. She'd been out of her depth going in—and she had *known* it. Just her luck to run into an "alpha" male on this relatively small island. Clash of the Titans, indeed. She was a very small Titan compared to Hawke.

Things were happening much too fast. She had a crazy impression of being inside a spiraling tunnel, rushing toward the bottom too rapidly to stop herself. And she didn't know what lay at the bottom.

Even supposing that Hawke had more in mind than a summer fling—and he'd never hinted that he did—what then? In the fairy tales it was always phrased "And they lived happily ever after." But Kendall had always wondered what happened after the story was ended.

Silly thing for a grown woman to wonder. But perhaps the question grew out of the years when Kendall had been learning about the real world at a time when other little girls had been playing with dolls and having tea parties.

And that was probably why Hawke's "storybook" romance was touching her so deeply. Having outgrown childish fantasies, few adults were granted the opportunity to wander through fairy tales and myths. But the little girl who had grown up too quickly still wondered what would happen when the romance came to an end.

On Wings of Magic

In a thoughtful mood Kendall got ready for dinner that night. She'd heard nothing from Hawke, and presumed that he hadn't yet returned from his trip. She had a feeling, though, that he would show up sometime that night.

With that in mind she studied her wardrobe carefully. Closing her ears to the little voice warning that she'd be sorry, she chose the sexiest dress in her closet. It was made of shimmering material, blue-green in color, and made her eyes look as changeable and mysterious as the sea. The skirt was open in the front nearly to her thighs. And the dress itself . . . it was backless, and two narrow straps rose from the waist to barely cover the tips of her breasts. The resulting plunging neckline plunged all the way to her navel.

And it took nerve to wear.

Kendall was fumbling with the clasp at her neck when she heard a slight sound from the suite next door. She wandered slowly into the sitting room of her own suite and stared at the connecting door, biting her lip.

Forever afterward, Kendall blamed her next impulse on sheer insanity.

Without giving herself time to think, she crossed the room and flung open the connecting door. Holding the straps of her dress in place, she stepped into Hawke's sitting room, calling lightly, "Hawke, would you—"

And stopped dead in her tracks.

The woman turning to face her was beautiful with the kind

of beauty one knew instinctively would never fade. Her dark hair was just beginning to gray at the temples, and her complexion was as clear and unlined as that of a woman thirty years her junior.

She was dressed with taste and elegance, her blue gown molding a slender figure that many a younger woman would have envied. And gray eyes just exactly like Hawke's regarded Kendall in a shrewd, amused appraisal.

Kendall knew . . . she *knew*.

If she'd been asked to name all the people in the world whose respect she would most like to have, this woman would have ranked high on the list. It didn't take a sixth sense to tell Kendall who she was.

It was all Hawke's fault, she decided numbly. Even when he wasn't around, he got her into trouble. And here she stood, holding up her skimpy dress while facing . . .

"Hello—you must be Kendall." The lovely woman smiled gently. "I've heard a great deal about you. I'm Sarah Madison —Hawke's mother."

Chapter

6

endall wished miserably that a Florida sinkhole would migrate south and swallow her up. Clutching her dress and her dignity, she managed a choked "Hi."

"Here, let me do that." The older woman stepped over to fasten Kendall's dress. "There."

"Thank you." Gathering her scattered wits, she went on. "I'm sorry for bursting in on you, Mrs. Madison, but I thought—" Her voice broke off abruptly as she realized that her thoughts had been painfully clear. And damning.

"Sarah, my dear." Hawke's mother seemed amused. "And it's quite all right. Hawke isn't back yet, I'm afraid." She led her reluctant guest to the sofa and indicated that she should sit down. "It will give us a chance to talk."

At the moment that was the last thing Kendall wanted. But she sat. "You've . . . spoken to Hawke?" she ventured.

"Several days ago. Just after you arrived here, I believe. He mentioned you then. And since I was in the area, I decided to stop by and meet you." She smiled easily. "Just a flying visit, I'm afraid; I'm on my way to Miami."

Kendall tried to relax. "Really? A vacation?"

"I was visiting relatives in Key West, and decided I'd had just about enough. So now I'm going home. I live in Miami."

"I see." But she didn't, really. From Key West to Miami via the Bahamas? The question was pushed aside, however, by another one. What had Hawke told his mother about her? And how could she find out without disgracing herself further?

"I'm so glad to have this chance to meet you," Hawke's mother was going on cheerfully. "Not that my approval would matter one way or the other to Hawke, but a mother likes to be *sure.*"

Kendall felt as if she'd been kicked in the stomach. "Mrs. Madison, I—"

"Sarah, please."

"*Sarah,*" Kendall began desperately, "I don't want you to get the wrong idea about—about my relationship with Hawke. We only met a few days ago, and we hardly know each other!"

Sarah's gray eyes gleamed with amusement. "I can see he's been giving you a hard time. Rick told me about the gifts; my son is more romantic than I'd suspected, it seems."

Kendall felt a flush creeping up her cheeks and fought to control it. "It's just a game to him," she muttered, rapidly going beyond the point of caring whom she was talking to.

"Tell me," Sarah pressed softly, and Kendall knew then where Hawke had gotten his uncanny gift of persuasion.

To her own astonishment she found herself talking earnestly to his mother.

"He told me not an hour after we'd met that he was going to sweep me off my feet—and he did. Literally. He carried me through the lobby, through a bar. He sends me absurd presents. And now he's got Rick watching over me while he's gone! The entire hotel's talking about me."

Sarah sat back and regarded Kendall thoughtfully. Then, in a bewildering change of subject, she said, "Tell me about yourself, my dear. Your parents, your childhood."

Strangely, Kendall found that it didn't feel at all wrong to be talking about her life to a woman she'd just met. She told Hawke's mother about the past fifteen rootless years, touching briefly on both the good times and the bad. And Sarah drew her out, inserting a soft question now and then, or a comment.

When Kendall finally finished speaking, the older woman looked at her carefully. "Have you ever wished for a home of your own? Asked yourself if you wanted to live out of suitcases for the rest of your life?"

"Sure." Kendall shrugged. "And I suppose I'll settle down one day. I don't know when, though, or where."

Sarah got to her feet, saying briskly, "Will you have dinner with me, Kendall?"

"Of course. Thank you." Kendall rose, fighting an urge to

tug at her all-too-brief dress. She excused herself long enough to go into her own suite and get her purse, then accompanied Hawke's mother down to the dining room.

Rick, apparently not surprised to see them together, joined them in the lobby and escorted them to the dining room. He waved away the headwaiter and showed them to a table personally.

Kendall saw the red envelope lying at her place, but she didn't open it until Rick had bowed solemnly and left them. Then, conscious of Sarah's smiling gaze, she opened the envelope. She pulled out a somewhat gaudy-looking valentine card, opened it, and read it silently. A soft flush spread over her cheeks, and she muttered, "It's a game. Just a game."

"If I wouldn't be prying . . ." Sarah began hesitantly.

Kendall handed her the card and busied herself unfolding her napkin. She wouldn't let herself think.

" 'Come live with me and be my love,' " Sarah recited softly. She looked steadily across the table at Kendall as she gave back the card. "It doesn't sound like a game."

"It is," Kendall murmured. "It has to be." She placed the card in her purse and hastily picked up a menu. "I'm starved," she told her companion brightly, then added in spite of herself, "You see how he embarrasses me?"

"Turn the tables on him," the older woman suggested mischievously. "Embarrass *him.*"

"I'd almost kill for the chance to do that," Kendall responded wryly. "But how? Nothing seems to rattle him."

Sarah looked thoughtful, and remained so until their waiter had come and taken their orders. Then, watching the retreating red back, she said, "Ask him about the peculiar scar he has."

"Scar?" Kendall had a feeling that Sarah wasn't talking about the scar on Hawke's shoulder.

And she wasn't.

By the time the waiter returned with their first course, Kendall was giggling helplessly and Sarah wore an expression that was strictly woman-to-woman. An expression women down through the ages had worn while busily plotting the downfall of a man.

A little breathlessly Kendall managed to say, "I wouldn't dare ask him about that! He'd kill me if anyone else heard!"

"Perhaps." Sarah smiled slightly as she picked up her fork. "But I think you could get away with it. Pick a public place and ask him discreetly—so that only the two of you know what you mean."

Kendall giggled again. "You mean—so that only the two of us know where it is!"

Sarah laughed. "Exactly."

Picking up her fork, Kendall said wistfully, "Just to see his face!"

Kendall enjoyed the meal. Thoroughly. She pushed the

meaning of Hawke's most recent gesture from her mind and just talked to his mother. Sarah was a fascinating woman, well educated and well traveled, and a born storyteller. And Kendall was honestly delighted to have met her—in spite of the less-than-dignified meeting.

After dinner both decided on an early night, and walked together to the elevator. Sarah stopped the car on the fifth floor, telling Kendall that her room was there, and causing the younger woman to apologize for having taken her suite. But Sarah only laughed.

"Nonsense, my dear! I don't care which room I sleep in for a single night. I'll be leaving the island tomorrow afternoon, so we'll have a chance to talk tomorrow morning. See you then."

Kendall nodded and, in a thoughtful mood, rode the rest of the way to her floor alone. She wondered vaguely why Sarah hadn't chosen to use Hawke's suite for the night, then dismissed the question. Having reached her floor, she left the elevator and walked to the door of her suite, fishing for her keys in her purse.

She unlocked her door and went inside, automatically flipping on the lights as she turned to fasten the night chain. She dropped her purse on the desk by the door, then kicked off her shoes and turned back to the room. And froze.

Gypsy was lying on the couch, staring suspiciously at the new objects resting on the coffee table. Kendall walked over

slowly to the table and stared down, a sound somewhere between a shaky laugh and a groan escaping her lips.

The largest object was a castle colored from a dream in
soft pastel colors, and exquisitely made out of wax. Each turret
was topped with a wick. It was a candle—several candles—and
utterly beautiful as it burned.

Beside the castle was a satin pillow, and on it rested a
crown. A tiara. It looked very old and very delicate, like a web
spun of fine gold. If Kendall hadn't told herself firmly that it
couldn't possibly be real, she would have suspected that the
center setting was a large ruby and the surrounding ones diamonds. But, of course, it couldn't be real.

She bent slowly and picked up the tiara, turning it in her
hands for a moment. He wasn't being fair, she thought dimly.
He wasn't being fair at all. How was she supposed to fight this
sort of thing? Holding the tiara, she went back to the desk and
stared at her reflection in the mirror above it.

Feeling a little like a fool but unable to resist the impulse,
she placed the tiara carefully on her head. It looked . . . right
somehow, nestled in her silvery hair. The rubylike stone
gleamed dully and the diamonds glittered.

Crowns and castles. Seashells, wind chimes, suncatchers,
and . . . unicorns. He called it romance. Kendall didn't know
what to call it, but she was very much afraid that it wasn't real.
She had a peculiar feeling that if she'd only pinch herself hard
enough, she'd wake up.

The question was—did she want to wake up?

He wasn't giving her time to think this through, that was the problem. And storybook romance was so utterly alien to everything she'd ever known, it wasn't easy to deal with.

She had another of those peculiar feelings. This wasn't happening to her. Someone else was receiving these lovely presents, and trying to cope with a man unlike any she'd ever known before. Someone else was standing before a mirror, thinking about Alice in Wonderland, and wondering if maybe she'd stumbled into someone's strange dream. A strange and magical dream.

Because things like this just didn't *happen* to Kendall James. She was a woman of reality, and knew better than to indulge herself with fairy tales. She had seen too much to be innocent. And she just couldn't understand why a man she'd met only days before would be surrounding her with a dream she couldn't believe in.

It had to be a game. But what was the point of the game, and what were the rules? What would she win if she won? And what would she lose if she lost?

Some slight noise drew her attention from the mirror, and she looked up to see Hawke step through the connecting door and into her suite. He looked a bit tired, and was dressed in a casual shirt unbuttoned to the waist and dark slacks. And his gray eyes gleamed as they moved slowly from the glittering tiara to the bare toes peeking out from the hem of her sexy blue-green dress.

"A crown for a princess," he murmured almost inaudibly.

Kendall swallowed hard and tried to think straight, almost overwhelmed by a sudden urge to reach out and touch him. It was like a hunger, a need stronger than any she'd felt before. So strong that it was frightening.

"I—you shouldn't keep giving me presents," she managed to say weakly.

"I like to," he responded simply.

She tore her eyes away from the gray ones holding her as if in a spell, and glanced toward the burning castle. "They're beautiful. All of them. But—"

"No buts." He took a step closer to her. "I wanted to chase the sadness from your eyes, to make you laugh. Did I do that, honey?" His voice was quiet, almost hushed.

Kendall fought a desire to fling herself into his arms, keeping her hands rigidly at her sides. Unable to lie to him, she said, "You made me laugh. And swear at you."

He smiled as her eyes returned to his, fully understanding that last wry statement. Crossing the room to stand before her, he brought a small, gaily wrapped package from behind his back and handed it to her gravely.

She gave him a helpless look. "Hawke, you can't—"

"Open it."

Sighing, Kendall unwrapped the gift and folded back the

tissue paper inside. She gasped softly as she stared down at the small porcelain bell. The handle was a child angel, with a halo and delicate wings. The robes of the angel were the bowl of the bell, and a minute sash of wildflowers ringed the tiny waist and hung down the front of the robes. A dark child angel, with huge brown eyes and a smile as sweet as sunshine.

"It—looks like Rosita," she whispered, removing the bell from its box and then staring up at Hawke with dazed eyes.

"I hoped it would." He smiled faintly. "It wasn't easy to find a dark angel. Most of them are blond and blue-eyed." Almost compulsively, he reached out to touch her soft hair. "Even the real ones."

Holding the delicate angel in her hands, Kendall gazed up at him. She saw the rather hard face soften, and realized that she had badly misjudged him by believing that her confession had meant nothing to him. "You didn't say anything the next day," she whispered. "About Rosita."

His hands clasped her shoulders gently. "No. After going over it all the night before, I was afraid that mentioning Rosita would upset you. I wanted to make you laugh."

Kendall smiled. "Or make me angry?"

There was a responsive gleam in his gray eyes. "Well, if you're snapping at me, you can't be sad."

She looked back down at the bell, her smile dying. "It's a beautiful gift, Hawke. Thank you."

"You're very welcome." Hawke's voice dropped suddenly

to a husky note. "It's a magic bell, Kendall. When you ring it, it will always bring you a hawk."

Kendall stood perfectly still as he lifted the bell from her nerveless fingers and set it gently on the desk. She felt the breath catch in her throat when his hands returned to warmly cup her face, turning it up. There was a look of intensity in his eyes that she had never seen before, touching the woman in her.

"These past three days have been hell," he said softly, his breath warm on her upturned face. "I picked up the phone a dozen times to call you, just to hear your voice. God, Kendall—"

When his lips touched hers, she gave an almost inaudible sigh and slipped her arms around his lean waist. It wouldn't hurt, a part of her whispered, to be in his arms for a while. Just a while. Something inside of her needed the touch of him.

His hands slid down abruptly, molding her slender hips and pulling her lower body against his. And then he tore his mouth away with an obvious effort. "Kendall—"

Silently, Kendall rose on her toes, pressing her lips to his and cutting off whatever he'd meant to say. She wasn't interested in words right now. She didn't want to talk and she didn't want to think. All she wanted was for this moment to go on forever.

Immediately, Hawke's arms tightened around her and his lips hardened in a sudden demanding force. There was undisguised hunger in his kiss, and a drugging power that sapped the strength from Kendall's legs. She responded to him mindlessly, pressing her body against his until the thunder of his heart felt like her own.

Never in her life had she experienced anything like this. She felt as if she were on fire, burning with a primitive hunger that threatened to escape the frail human container holding it.

Hawke's mouth burned a trail down her throat, settling at last on the golden curve of her breast left bare by the plunging neckline of her dress. "You don't know what you're doing to me," he grated softly, one hand sliding up to cup her breast through the silky dress.

Kendall dug her nails into his back, gasping as she felt his mouth move hotly against her skin. "I don't care what I'm doing," she murmured huskily, feeling his free hand move to the clasp of her dress.

There was a whisper of sound, and the dress slid to the floor, leaving Kendall wearing only a pair of very brief white panties—and a crown. He swept her up into his arms and carried her into the bedroom, placing her gently on the turned-down bed and lowering his weight beside her.

Smoky gray eyes moved slowly over her bare flesh, and Kendall felt a peculiar heady excitement at the knowledge that he found her body beautiful. She tugged the shirt from the waistband of his pants, snapping the last button in her impatience as she pushed the garment from his shoulders.

He shrugged it to the floor, then lifted the tiara from her head and placed it on the nightstand, where a lamp burned. Strong fingers raked gently through her hair, sending pins flying, and then his mouth was moving hungrily on hers.

Kendall gave herself up totally to the sensations he was arousing in her. Her tongue met his, tasting and exploring; her fingers probed the length of his spine. She shivered when his hand moved caressingly over her flat belly; moaned when his lips left hers to capture a hardening nipple.

"So beautiful," he muttered hoarsely, using his lips and teeth sensuously to bring her desire to a fever pitch. "Touch me, Cinderella . . . your touch is magic."

Eagerly, Kendall obeyed the command, her hands moving over his lean ribs, exploring the muscled chest and back. But when her fingers discovered his belt buckle, a strong hand covered hers, stopping her impatient attempt to do away with another barrier.

He raised his head, breathing roughly, the gray eyes dark and feverish. "Do you love me, Kendall?" he demanded.

Turquoise eyes blinked in confusion as she stared up at him. "Don't ask me that now," she practically wailed.

"What better time is there?" He trapped her restless legs with one of his, capturing her free hand as it tried vainly to wander again. "I'm making love to you, honey. I want to know if you love me."

Kendall wasn't thinking very clearly, but she wasn't about

to commit herself to a man she'd known less than a week. It didn't strike her—then—that she had been willing to make a commitment far deeper than any verbal promise could ever be. "Hawke, please!" She tried to free her hands from his grasp and failed.

"Answer me, Kendall."

Desire faded slowly as she stared up at him, and her body ached with an emptiness that was frightening. Stubbornly, she remained silent.

"I could take you right now, couldn't I?" His voice was still rough, the gray eyes hooded now. "But you wouldn't belong to me. Everything you have to give is still locked inside that beautiful, stubborn head."

Kendall felt a sudden surge of an unfamiliar yearning emotion. Closing her mind to his words, she lifted her head suddenly from the pillow and pressed her lips to his with a hunger that dimly astonished her. There was someone inside her head, crying out to him silently to take her, to make her his before she had time to think, before she could convince herself that this was wrong.

Hawke groaned deep in his chest and returned the kiss eagerly for a timeless moment, then wrenched his mouth from hers and rolled away to sit on the edge of the bed. In a low, gritty voice containing an odd thread of humor, he muttered, "I am certifiably out of my mind."

Blankly, Kendall watched as he bent to get his shirt from

the floor and then rose to his feet. "Hawke? Where are you going?" Her voice very nearly squeaked with incredulity.

He half turned to stare down at her. "Well, I have three choices." The slow, measured tone didn't quite hide the hoarseness in his voice. "A dip in the ocean, the pool, or a cold shower."

Whispering, she asked, "What about the fourth choice?"

His face tightened and he started determinedly for the door. Over his shoulder, he told her, "I'm trying—desperately —not to think of the fourth, Kendall."

"But, Hawke . . ." Her voice halted him at the door. "I —I want you to stay."

His hand came out to grasp the doorjamb, and Kendall watched the knuckles whiten. Then he turned to gaze across the room at her, the gray eyes intense again. "It's not enough, Kendall." At her startled look, his mouth twisted slightly. "I know. Like I said—I'm out of my mind. I should take what you're offering and be satisfied with it. But I want more."

Confused thoughts jostled one another in Kendall's mind, and she could only say weakly, "But I thought you said that you wanted only a summer romance."

"I never said that, honey." His voice was very quiet. "You did."

Kendall was still staring at the empty doorway when she heard the connecting door to his suite close softly. With near-hysterical hindsight, she told herself that she should have demanded a lock for that damned door the very first day. The way he waltzed in and out of her "private" suite was ludicrous.

Various emotions jostled for precedence within her, and the winning feeling was sheer frustration. Her body was aching, and she had just literally thrown herself at a man who had somewhat cryptically refused her, stating that he wanted more.

More? Well, that made a hell of a lot of sense! It did, really, but she didn't like to think about the sense it made. He'd demanded if she loved him, had more or less implied that he wanted her to belong to him.

Kendall knew what that meant. Commitment. He wanted her to commit herself to him. But she wasn't ready for that. If nothing else, she barely knew the man! True, he was presently indulging in a quixotic fit of romance, but how long would that last? She could very well wake up one day and find herself committed to a stranger.

And exactly what kind of commitment did he want from her? Just—just!—a confession of love? An affair? Marriage? Sarah, she remembered suddenly, had implied that she knew her son had chosen his future wife, and that even before the episode of the crown and castle.

She rolled onto her side and stared at the glittering tiara on the nightstand. The symbolism was obvious, though a bit elaborate. A castle and crown for a princess. And one did not, she decided with vague reluctance, present a crown to a—what was the term?—oh, yes. Paramour.

And the gaudy valentine bearing the quotation "Come live with me and be my love."

Dammit. How was she supposed to keep a clear head while being bombarded with that sort of thing? A sneering little voice in her head warned that if she wasn't careful, she'd wake up one day to find that the handsome prince had turned into a frog.

Ignoring the fact that she was almost naked, Kendall rolled off the bed and went into her sitting room. Then, very carefully, she got the chair from her desk and wedged it beneath the doorknob of the connecting door. Probably a totally useless gesture. When one owned a hotel, it was doubtful that locked doors could stand against one.

But it made her feel slightly better.

She paused long enough to blow out the candle. She stared at the tiny bell, then picked it up and took it into the bedroom. Setting it gently on the nightstand beside the tiara, she stared at both for a moment, then sighed and went into the bathroom to take a shower. A cold shower.

A little while later she went back into the bedroom wearing a sheer shortie nightgown and climbed into bed, muttering to herself. She'd found a faint bruise at the base of her neck while brushing her hair before the vanity mirror. Terrific. Another symbol of bondage to parade in front of the royal subjects.

Choking back a giggle, Kendall settled back on her pillow

and stared fixedly at the ceiling. And admitted silently that it was time for a little soul-searching.

Even though she felt nervous at having known him such a short time, she knew that there was a deeper reason why she wanted to avoid committing herself to Hawke. And that reason was sheer fear. In her mind the commitment of love between a man and a woman was the deepest possible bond. It was the reason she had never indulged in the shallow surface relationships that were apparently a worldwide epidemic. Love was a final thing, a giving of oneself to someone else. And she had seen too little love in the world to bestow her own carelessly.

So . . . if she admitted to Hawke that she loved him, she would be burning her bridges. There would be no chance of escaping without pain if Hawke decided he'd made a mistake.

Suddenly, Kendall sat bolt upright on the bed, her eyes wide and startled as she stared across the room. *If she admitted . . . !* Oh, God—it was too late. She was head over heels in love with a man she'd met less than a week before.

And the funny thing was . . . she hadn't fallen in love with the handsome prince showering her with gifts and surrounding her with romance. She had fallen in love with the man who had looked down at her with pain and understanding in his eyes and vulnerability in his face. The man who had understood her grief at the death of a child she had loved. The man who had soothed her after a nightmare.

All her life she'd been locked inside a hellish cocoon of cool self-reliance and independence. Her father loved her, but he was a busy man, and she had learned to take care of herself. She had never in her life transferred her burdens to someone else's shoulders.

She wanted to now.

Kendall lay back slowly on the pillow, and then turned on her side to stare at the tiara and angel bell on the nightstand. Two sides of the man, she thought dimly. A mind that could conceive of an absurd romance, sending "his" lady a crown. And the same mind sensitively giving another kind of gift, one that would always represent a special memory.

God . . . if she could only be *sure!* But she was still afraid. Afraid of giving up so much of herself on an impossible chance. Afraid of loving and losing.

And she wished vaguely that Hawke had taken her before she had had the chance to think. It would have been much simpler.

The wish set up a train of thought, and Kendall frowned slightly as she stared at the gifts. Why was Hawke so intent on hearing her commit herself? Usually it was the woman who demanded at least a verbal promise of love before commitment and consummation. Just her luck to stumble on a man secure enough to switch roles. *He* wanted commitment. *He* wanted love.

Why? Did he love her? Or was it simply the conquering instinct? No. There was nothing even remotely simple about Hawke Madison. Which was why she couldn't believe that he loved her. It was too simple.

Rolling over onto her back, Kendall stared restlessly at the ceiling. She was sorely tempted to cast all of her questions and doubts into the sea and just follow her instincts—which would have meant going to Hawke right now, this minute. And to hell with tomorrow.

But she couldn't do that. Kendall had had very little experience with fantasy in her life. Reality, though . . . reality she knew very well. She hugged her empty belly and stared upward, refusing to gaze again at the little angel on the nightstand.

The pain had eased, but the memory would always be there. She had loved Rosita, loved her enough so that she had been making arrangements to adopt her. Dreams. Killed by reality. And a part of her had died with the little girl she had loved.

Another loss like that one would destroy her, she knew. And if she gave her love to Hawke and lost . . . It didn't bear thinking of. Kendall closed her mind to thought. She was getting nowhere by going over and over this. Logically, there was no way out, and thinking about it wouldn't suddenly disclose an escape hatch, she knew. And the stakes were far too high to gamble.

Kendall reached over to turn off the lamp, keeping her eyes averted from the bell and tiara. Then she settled back on her pillow and stared at darkness, muttering forlornly to the empty room, "There's a lot to be said for good old-fashioned lust. . . ."

C h a p t e r

9

When Kendall stepped out of the elevator early the next morning, she was wearing short shorts and a halter top that quite probably would get her arrested. The outfit was so brief that it immediately convinced one hotel guest that she was wearing nothing but golden flesh. He promptly tripped over a potted plant in the lobby.

She heard the resulting thump, but since, in her mind, she was wearing battle armor, Kendall didn't connect the noise with herself. She strolled across the lobby and stared at Rick for a moment. "Your mouth is open."

His mouth snapped shut. "Is that a bikini?"

"No." Kendall glanced down and noted absently that her top provided very little except moral support. She looked back at the manager. "Is Sarah down yet?"

Rick shook his head, still looking a bit stunned.

Kendall sighed. "Well, I'm going for a walk on the beach. Tell her that if she comes down before I get back."

"Okay. Kendall," he added as she went to turn away, "do you want me to put that tiara in the hotel safe? Not that I think it would get stolen, but if it would make you feel better . . ."

Her blank look slowly changed to one of comprehension, and her voice emerged unsteadily. "You mean—it's real?"

Disconcerted, Rick muttered, "I thought Hawke had—oh, damn. I really blew it, didn't I?"

Ignoring the wry comment, Kendall said, "It's on the nightstand in my bedroom." She was a little pale, but in control. "Please send someone up to get it. Then see that Hawke gets it back."

"He won't take it back." Rick was obviously disgusted with himself for having let the cat out of the bag.

"Then put it in the safe!" She lowered her voice with an effort, then asked quietly, "Is it an heirloom?"

The manager immediately looked uneasy. "You'll have to ask Hawke. It was his present."

"I'm asking you."

"Pass. I've already put my foot in my mouth once today, thank you. Twice would be a habit."

Kendall decided to be angry. It was a very sane and carefully thought-out decision. Hawke had said that if she was snapping at him, she couldn't be sad. It wouldn't be easy to be passionate either, she thought. So she'd be angry. And snap a lot. And maybe—just maybe—he'd never know that she loved him.

"Where is he?"

Rick shrugged and gave a hands-out gesture of innocence. "Beats me. I haven't seen him this morning."

"Male solidarity." When Rick only smiled charmingly, Kendall gave him a disgusted look and turned away. That was when she saw Hawke and the romantic-minded Amanda Foster emerge from the elevator.

"I want to talk to you!" Kendall threw the statement fiercely across the lobby, not particularly concerned—at this point—whether or not anyone overheard.

Hawke looked faintly surprised, but strolled across the lobby, devastatingly handsome in a full-sleeved black pirate-type shirt open to the waist, and black slacks. The shirt prompted a thought in Kendall's mind; she thought she knew now where the tiara had come from.

Amanda Foster became suddenly fascinated by the potted palm that Kendall's earlier admirer had fallen over.

"Just what do you mean," Kendall demanded as Hawke reached her, "by giving me a priceless tiara?"

Hawke looked over her shoulder at Rick, and Kendall heard the manager mutter a constricted "Sorry, boss." Whether the constriction came from embarrassment or laughter, she didn't know. Or care. With a sigh Hawke said, "Why don't we talk on the beach? You seem to be dressed for it."

"Why don't we talk here." She ignored the remark about her outfit.

He leaned an elbow on the desk and stared at her thoughtfully. "I wanted you to have the tiara. Period."

"I can't accept it, of course," she told him politely.

"You already have. In front of witnesses."

It was an unfortunate remark; it called to mind the sense of ill-usage Kendall had been feeling for the past few days. He'd very neatly thrown her off balance last night with the angel bell, to the point that she had forgotten everything else. Now she remembered.

In a voice ringing with frustration, she snapped, "You've been making a spectacle of me since the day I walked through those doors!" She gestured angrily toward the glass doors. "You've embarrassed me in front of all the guests—*and* your mother. I feel as if I'm walking around wearing a sign that says SOLD!"

"I thought it was a scarlet *A.*"

The amused remark added fuel to what was already a raging fire. Kendall had gotten very little sleep the night before, and she was never at her best early in the morning. And, of course, she'd already decided to be angry.

Very quietly, and with a certain amount of artistic skill, she swore at him in four languages. Not giving a particular damn whether or not he understood, she tore his character to shreds, cast impolite aspersions on his integrity, threw his ancestry into a very uncertain light, and shot holes into his general claim to humanity. The only thing she missed calling him was a horse thief—and that was an oversight.

Rick was choking suspiciously behind the desk; Amanda Foster was looking faintly shocked; Hawke was listening courteously.

When she'd finally run down, the man to whom the discourse had been addressed looked at Rick and said mildly, "Regular little spitfire, isn't she?"

"Dammit, Hawke—"

He leaned over and kissed her. Firmly.

"Stop that! You—"

He kissed her again. Even more firmly.

"I *can't* accept—"

And again. One hand traced down her bare spine.

"Hawke!" It was a wail.

This time his hands found her tiny waist.

"Oh . . . hell." Kendall felt her arms creep up around his neck. Her body wouldn't let her do anything else. Damn the man; he knew all the right buttons to push.

When he at last drew away—still keeping his hands at her waist—Kendall blinked at him. "You are an unscrupulous man," she told him seriously.

"I know." His voice was comforting.

"This doesn't mean a thing, you know. I'm still mad at you."

"I know."

She sighed and absently locked her fingers together behind his neck. "You can't keep giving me these absurd presents. Crowns and castles and unicorns. This isn't a fairy tale."

"Of course it is. Romance."

She ignored that. "I won't keep them."

"Yes, you will."

"Not the tiara."

"Especially the tiara."

"No." She hastily hid her face against his chest when he would have kissed her. "I won't," she told him in a muffled voice. "I just won't." Unexpectedly, the clean male scent of him made her senses reel, and she quickly lifted her head.

He was smiling down at her strangely. "Since I won't take it back, you'll have to keep it, won't you?"

Kendall gave him a despairing look. "Do you have to have everything your own way?"

"Everything. Now, thank me for the nice presents." He swatted her lightly on the bottom, causing her to jump in surprise.

"I already thanked you," she muttered, ruefully aware that she was giving in to him again.

"You thanked me for the seashells and the bell—not the rest. Be a good girl and thank me properly."

Kendall stared up at him, accurately reading the gleam in

his gray eyes. And hastily looked away from the magnetic command there. If he thought she was going to kiss him . . . Swallowing hard, she got out a carefully polite "Thank you very much."

"Not good enough."

"What do you want—blood?" she snapped, suddenly remembering that she was supposed to be angry.

"Just a kiss. Freely given."

She saw that her arms were still around his neck, and quickly lowered them to push uselessly against his chest. "No!" With another surge of despair she realized that the little scene had attracted more observers. Why couldn't the guests in this hotel sleep late like normal human beings, for God's sake?

"Come on, honey—one little kiss. It won't hurt you."

The reproachful tone did nothing for Kendall's state of mind. But she had no intention of giving in to him on this. It was high time that Hawke Madison learned he couldn't have everything his own way! "Let go of me."

"No," he replied with shattering simplicity.

If Kendall had been given to screaming, she would have rattled the hotel from cellar to rafters. And then, suddenly, her mind began to work. A calculating gleam entered her blue-green eyes, and she knew then how she could even several scores—*and* end this embarrassing little scene.

She drew a coaxing finger down the opening of his shirt, fiercely closing her mind to the sensation it produced in her nerve endings. "Hawke . . . I'll do as you ask. *If* you'll answer one question for me. Truthfully."

"Sure." The answer was immediate, but his tone was a little guarded. And the gray eyes had narrowed slightly, suspiciously.

Kendall deliberately raised her voice so that the onlookers would hear the question. *Sauce for the gander!* she reminded herself silently. "Where did you get that funny little scar? The one shaped like the marks of someone's teeth? You know, the one on your—"

"Kendall!"

He looked more rattled than she had ever seen him, a tide of red creeping up under the tanned flesh of his cheeks. His hands fell away from her and he cast a swift, startled look around the lobby.

She carefully backed away a couple of steps and smiled at him sweetly. Sending a silent, gleeful thanks to Sarah, she said sadly, "You're not going to answer? What a pity. And I was so curious too. Bye, now." She turned and casually left the lobby.

It was a magnificent exit, completely victorious and leaving behind a silence broken only by Rick's choking laughter.

Kendall held on to her serene expression until she reached the virtually deserted beach. Then, giggling, she began to run, enjoying the morning and exhilarated by her successful display of one-upmanship. There would probably be retaliation, but she wasn't particularly concerned with that possibility right now. She just wanted to enjoy her triumph for a while.

She ran for a while—a casual habit with her—and then went back to the hotel. Like a wary child, she peered into the lobby until she satisfied herself that neither Hawke nor Rick was there, then made a dash for the elevator. Reaching her suite without incident, she took a shower and put on a cool summer dress.

Ten minutes later she was having breakfast in the dining room with Sarah. The older woman cheerfully told her that she hadn't seen Hawke that morning, and Kendall didn't mention the scene in the lobby.

Hawke showed up halfway through the meal, with a gleam in his eye and a very bland manner. He somehow made it impossible for Kendall to excuse herself gracefully, talking casually to both her and his mother.

Sarah seemed highly amused.

When Kendall finally decided to ignore manners and just *go,* he caught her wrist firmly and invited her gently to sit down again. She sat. There was something very unnerving about that gleam. Silently, she listened to him arguing quietly with Sarah about seeing her off that afternoon; she insisted that she needed no company on the helicopter trip to Nassau, and he maintained that she did.

Sarah won the argument. She also insisted that the two of them need not bother to entertain her, since she had decided to

fly to Nassau a little earlier than planned. She was sure they had
things to do.

Somewhat to her surprise, Kendall discovered that they
did. They left Sarah enjoying her coffee in the dining room, and
Hawke maintained his grip on her wrist until they were in the
lobby.

"You run up to your room and change, honey," he told
her cheerfully, releasing her wrist at last.

"Change into what?" she bristled, staring at him.

"Something casual. And you might want to wear a bathing
suit underneath. Don't forget rubber-soled shoes."

Kendall frowned at him. "What have you got in mind?"

"We're going sailing."

"Oh, *are* we?"

"Yes." He gave her a gentle push toward the elevator and
a swat on the bottom—again. "You can even bring the cat,
since she apparently likes to swim. I need to get to know her,
anyway."

"You don't need to know Gypsy, and I—"

Hawke sighed. "If you don't run up and change, honey,
I'll take you to the boat just the way you are."

Kendall considered challenging that statement . . . except that she knew he would. Damn him. Giving him a goaded
look, she turned away, suffering the indignity of another swat
with nothing more than an irritated mutter.

"Be back down here in ten minutes." He sounded amused.

"Yes, master." She made the reply sarcastic, but as she got in the elevator and heard him laughing, she wondered if it was truer than she wanted to admit to herself. Hastily, she shunted the thought aside. No more soul-searching; she was still raw from the last time.

She was back down in nine minutes, wearing cutoff jeans and a colorful T-shirt over a bikini, and carrying her beachbag. With her cat draped around her neck.

Hawke took her wrist again and began leading her toward the door, and when she protested that she hadn't said good-bye to Sarah, told her easily, "You'll see Mother again."

The promise left Kendall silent and uneasy.

Hawke drove one of the hotel jeeps to the south end of the island, where a small marina lay. About a score of small boats were berthed there, mostly sailboats of various size.

Ignoring Gypsy's mutters of dislike, Hawke got out after parking the jeep and came around to help Kendall. "Your cat doesn't like me," he observed wryly.

Watching him retrieve a large wicker hamper from the back of the jeep, Kendall said calmly, "Because of that first morning. You fished her out of a bathtub and she hates to have her bath interrupted."

Hawke stared at her for a moment, then at the yellow-eyed

cat. "Hitching my fate to a couple of spitfires," he murmured. "I ought to have my head examined."

Before Kendall could respond—fortunately—he took her arm and began leading her toward the boats. The one he finally stopped beside was a twenty-foot beauty. Without comment she allowed him to help her over the side.

He stowed the hamper below, then returned to stare consideringly at Kendall. "Do you know boats?"

"Yes." She didn't elaborate.

"Good," he said briskly. "Then you can take the wheel." He stripped off the black slacks to reveal a pair of white swim trunks, leaving the pirate shirt on. "Will Gypsy do anything cute—like try climbing the sails—if you turn her loose?"

"No." A smile tugged at her lips for the first time. "Gypsy knows boats too."

An answering smile gleamed in his eyes. "Then by all means, let her loose." He busied himself making ready to sail.

Deciding to simply relax and enjoy herself, Kendall released her cat and then placed her beachbag out of their way, taking her seat behind the brass wheel. "Does the boat have a name?" she called out to Hawke, vaguely irritated with herself for her inability to keep her eyes off him. Particularly his legs. Damn.

He looked back at her in the act of raising the sails, grinning. "Of course. She's called the *Enchantress.*"

She might have known.

They were both somewhat caught up in getting the small craft out of the marina for some time. Once out, Hawke, rather to Kendall's surprise, didn't offer to take the wheel. Instead, he went below for a moment, returning with a small white pail.

Kendall looked at him uncertainly. "I don't know these waters, Hawke. Are there any reefs, or—"

He was shaking his head. "Not on this side of the island. Just keep heading due north." Sitting down cross-legged on the deck near the wheel, he opened the small pail and produced a piece of raw fish, which he gravely offered to Gypsy.

The cat, sitting at Kendall's feet, stared at the morsel rather disdainfully for a moment, then delicately accepted it. Hawke offered a second. Gypsy accepted it. And a third.

Trying to keep one eye on her steering and one eye on the little scene going on beside her, Kendall dutifully kept the boat heading in the right direction. Ten minutes later she heaved an inward sigh as she heard Gypsy giving her version of a purr—which sounded something like a large engine idling. Hawke had a friend for life. By the time they reached the northern end of the island, the cat was in his lap, blissfully having her chin scratched.

Hawke took over the wheel then, expertly swinging the small boat around the northern tip of the island and drifting east slightly before heading south.

Once they were on course, Kendall stripped off her jeans and T-shirt, revealing the tiny black bikini beneath. Bending over to get her sunglasses out of her bag, she asked dryly, "Did you invite Gypsy along just so you could seduce her with fish?"

"Something like that."

"It's only cupboard love, you know."

"Good enough. When it's a cat."

Kendall sat down on the padded seat beside the cabin door and lifted a brow at him. "As opposed to—?"

"A human. For instance," he went on blandly, "I'd hate for you to start loving me just because I fed you fish."

"What about diamonds and rubies?" she murmured, determined to take him lightly.

"That's a bit different. The tiara was given with a certain spirit—which I trust you appreciated."

Kendall bit the inside of her cheek to keep from laughing. "Oh, I appreciated the spirit. Everyone in the *hotel* appreciated the spirit."

He grinned at her pained tone. "Well, you have to admit —there can be no doubt about my intentions."

She hastily shoved the sunglasses onto her nose. "Where are we going, by the way?"

"Change of subject?" he muttered wryly, and then went on before she could respond. "Nowhere in particular. I thought you might want to see some of the other islands. Can you scuba dive?"

"Yes."

He grinned faintly and shot her an amused glance. "Stupid question. Is there anything you *haven't* done?"

"A few things." Kendall wasn't about to tell him the most important thing she hadn't done. He probably wouldn't have believed her anyway. Not that she could blame him. With her life-style, most people would have considered her virginity a miracle.

"Skydiving?" He cocked a quizzical brow.

"I've tried it." When he looked startled, Kendall laughed and added, "Not willingly."

He looked even more startled. "What?"

She sighed. "It's a long story."

"So? We have all day. And you can't leave me hanging like this!"

Kendall drew her legs up on the seat and watched Gypsy make herself comfortable at Hawke's feet. "Well, it was about five years ago. Daddy had an assignment in South America, and didn't want me to go. I was supposed to visit friends in the States. Anyway, I decided to go, so I—uh—stowed away on his plane."

"Good Lord," Hawke murmured faintly.

"Ummm. Daddy was a little more vocal about it. But the plane was in the air by then, so he couldn't very well shove me out the door. I'd gotten him smoothed down—barely—when the pilot announced that he was having engine trouble. And we were right over this godforsaken jungle, with no landing strip for miles.

"The pilot—not being the courageous sort—decided he'd rather not go down with his ship, and bailed out. And since the rest of us didn't know much about flying, we had no choice but to follow suit."

"What happened?" Hawke looked intrigued.

Kendall drew one knee up and rested her chin on it. "Well, we'd all had survival training, so we stayed alive. But we had to spend three horrible nights in that jungle. I woke up on the second morning to find a boa constrictor curled up beside me. It was nearly as big around as I was, and twenty-five feet long." Reflectively, she added, "I've been afraid of snakes ever since."

Hawke was staring at her. "You're kidding?"

She crossed her heart solemnly. "I swear."

His mouth twitched. "What happened to the boa?"

"I really don't know. I shut my eyes and started screaming. By the time Daddy got me calmed down, it was gone. Either I'd scared it off, or one of them had."

There was an odd expression in Hawke's eyes as he looked at her. "Tell me more."

Kendall shifted a little uneasily beneath that look. "It's almost always boring to hear someone else's adventures. Besides—it's all pretty tame."

"Climbing mountains, jumping out of planes and waking

up next to boa constrictors is tame?" He shook his head. "Really, Kendall, I'd like to hear about your life. And I doubt very much that I'll be bored at all."

Deciding finally that she'd rather talk about her life than have Hawke make more comments about his intentions, she obeyed his request. She touched lightly on various events in her life, most of them comical. Like the time the son of a diplomat had mischievously turned his pet mongoose loose in the middle of a diplomatic ball. And the time in Africa when she'd been adopted by a baby elephant, which insisted on following her everywhere she went just like a pet dog—and led to some very strange encounters. And the time in Arabia when she had unwittingly gotten herself locked in with a harem—and the diplomatic red tape her father had had to wade through to get her out.

Funny things. Things to keep Hawke chuckling softly at the wheel of the sailboat. Things to keep herself from thinking too much about him and how she felt about him.

Hawke finally piloted the boat into a small cove on one of the islands, and she scrambled forward to drop the sails. He dropped the anchor and then went below, answering Kendall's quizzical look with a succinct "Lunch!"

When he came back up, bearing the wicker hamper, she said uneasily, "Surely I haven't talked that long."

He grinned. "Of course not—sea air just makes me hungry. Besides, I enjoyed it."

Since she wasn't wearing a watch and couldn't read minds, she had to take his word on both counts. Unfolding the blanket he handed her, she spread it out on the cleared space behind the wheel and then knelt to examine the contents of the hamper. Sea air made her hungry too.

From the looks of it, he'd told the hotel cook that an army was going sailing. There was chicken, potato salad, rolls, cheese and crackers, various fruit. And a bottle of vintage wine—complete with two delicate goblets. Kendall examined the label on the wine bottle and raised an eyebrow at Hawke. "For a picnic?"

He grinned. "You know wine too, I see."

"I have a working knowledge." She frowned at him. "This should be opened on a special occasion."

"This is a special occasion." He produced a corkscrew and took the bottle away from her. "A certain young lady I know did a very good job of evening the score this morning."

Fighting back a giggle, Kendall began to prepare two plates. "Oh, really? Got her own back, did she?"

"I'll say." He poured the wine into the goblets and handed her one, gravely accepting the plate she handed him. "In fact, she embarrassed the hell out of a certain romantic hotelier."

Kendall smiled at him sweetly, and waited.

He sighed and abruptly reverted to first person. "I ought to turn you over my knee for that little stunt, honey." When she continued to regard him easily, his mouth twisted slightly.

"Except that I can't, can I? It wouldn't be fair. You were playing by my rules, after all."

She lifted her glass in a silent toast and sipped her wine, still smiling.

"You learn fast," he observed wryly, then winked at her and began eating.

Kendall followed suit, deciding that sooner or later she was going to ask him about the scar again. Sarah hadn't been able to tell her where he'd gotten it, and she *was* curious. But it took either anger or nerve to ask a man a question like that, and right now she had neither.

They talked casually while they ate, feeding Gypsy tidbits from time to time and just quietly enjoying the soft sounds of water lapping against the side of the boat. It was a companionable time, and Kendall had never felt so content.

Feeling sleepy after the meal, she lay back on the blanket and rested her head on a life jacket, deciding vaguely that she wasn't going to move again if she could help it. "You're spoiling me," she murmured lazily, hearing him pack away the remainder of lunch.

He stretched out beside her, raising himself on an elbow and reaching over to remove her sunglasses. Sleepy blue-green eyes gazed up at him. "I'd like to," he said, his voice dark, hypnotic. "I'd like to spoil you. Take care of you." His lips quirked slightly. "Keep all the gremlins at bay."

"Romance," she whispered, too sleepy and utterly boneless to protest the idea. "But I can take care of myself, Hawke."

"I know you can." He placed an arm across her waist and smiled down at her a little crookedly. Whimsically, he went on. "You're a little thing. Beautiful, delicate, and you look about as fierce as a week-old kitten. But strong. You've led a life that tested every gentle quality in you again and again. It should have hardened you, made you cold and cynical."

"It has," she murmured, thinking of her reluctance to love.

"No." He shook his head slowly. "You're still gentle. Even when you're angry, the gentleness is there. You could probably swear the devil out of hell—in six languages—and still be gentle. And you're right; you can take care of yourself."

His arm tightened slightly. "But I still want to take care of you. I want to surround you with beauty and romance. Bring you flowers and buy you silly presents. I want to make sure that you'll never be hurt the way you were in the past, that you'll never have nightmares again."

He leaned over and kissed her softly. It was a warm, drugging kiss, filled with gentleness and something else, something Kendall couldn't identify. She sighed contentedly and slipped her arms up around his neck, needing to touch him and not giving a particular damn—at that moment—about anything else.

Hawke made no demands. He continued to kiss her gently

on her lips, her nose, her eyes. Soft caresses no heavier than dew. If there was passion in him, he held it rigidly in check. He seemed almost to cherish her, his wine-scented breath sweet and warm on her face.

"Hawke?" she said, eyes closed and impossibly heavy.

"What is it, honey?"

"I loved your presents."

"I'm glad."

She sighed, threading her fingers through his hair to keep her heavy arms from falling away from him. "I was too mad to tell you in the lobby."

"I know." He laughed softly. "My fault. I shouldn't do that to you."

With sleepy wisdom she went on. "But you love it. Embarrassing me. Making me say absurd things in front of people."

He chuckled again. "I suppose."

"And carrying me."

"Definitely."

"You're a strange man. I thought so from the very first. In fact, I very nearly caught the first northbound sea gull and got out of here. But Gypsy gets airsick."

With a laugh in his voice, Hawke told her, "Go to sleep, honey. You're not even making sense."

Kendall felt her arms slipping from around his neck and decided dimly that maybe she should. She did.

CR ⚘

She woke to find the sun low in the sky and an awning stretched out above her and shading her body. Yawning, she stretched like a lazy cat. And discovered Hawke sitting at the wheel, watching her, Gypsy resting comfortably in his lap.

"Hi," she ventured to say, her voice a little thick.

"Hi." He smiled slightly. "Have a nice nap?"

Kendall peered at the sun and frowned. "I think it was more than a nap. Why did you let me sleep so long?"

Hawke set the cat down and got to his feet, stretching. Ignoring her question, he asked one of his own. "Would you like to go for a swim? I have some scuba gear below."

"I'd love to." She rose and looked thoughtfully at Gypsy. "Has she been over the side yet?"

"Once." Hawke grinned. "I let her swim for a while, then fished her out and dried her off."

Kendall sighed. "She tends to have more enthusiasm than sense. Remind me to tell you about the time she decided to go swimming in the Nile. And the Panama Canal."

Hawke laughed and went below to get the gear. When he came back, they got ready and then went over the side, both experienced divers. Hawke guided, since he knew the waters, and Kendall was content to follow him.

The cove was a treasure house of fish, and the underwater scene breathtakingly beautiful. Kendall had never gotten used to it, and hoped she never would. They stayed under the surface until it became difficult to see, and then headed for the boat.

After fishing Gypsy from the water again and removing their gear, they made ready to sail back to their island, talking about what they had seen and sharing previous diving experiences. Companionable.

Once under way, both fell silent, enjoying the sinking sun and the sights of other islands they passed. Kendall made herself comfortable where she could watch Hawke's profile, then reached silently into her beachbag for the sketch pad she carried.

It was a habit carried over from childhood, when she had tried to make a sketch of the places and people she had seen. It had always seemed better than a photograph, and never had she forgotten anything she had drawn.

Now, without attracting Hawke's attention, she began to sketch him. It should have been a difficult task because his face was so distinctive and carried such character. But it wasn't. Not to her.

Her fingers flew over the paper, drawing a face that was hard on the surface and unexpectedly sensitive beneath. An uncompromising jaw, high cheekbones, arrogant nose. The startling eyes. Black hair blown by sea breezes. Pirate shirt.

Kendall stared at the sketch for a moment, regretful that it was stark black and white with no colors. But maybe that was

best for this man. The starkness revealed the force of his character, the beauty of bone structure and features. Intelligence in
the high forehead, wit in the mobile brows.

But she couldn't draw the deep, rough voice. Or the
laugh. And she couldn't draw a clean masculine scent. Or the
gentle understanding after a nightmare. Or the taste of a wine-
sweet mouth.

Carefully, Kendall slid the sketchpad into her beachbag,
his image imprinted in her mind for all time.

Then she stared at the man.

C h a p t e r

I he next three days were companionable ones. Cheerfully ignoring her occasional weak protests, Hawke kept her busy from morning until late at night. They played tennis, swam, sailed, went diving. They even spent an uproarious afternoon trying their hand at windsurfing. Hawke was good at it, but Kendall spent more time in the water than on the board.

The nights were spent in various ways. He took her dancing—at both his hotels. They walked on the beach. One reckless night was spent in the casino, where Hawke staked Kendall and watched her win and lose a small fortune at blackjack. They sat in the bar and listened to music—where Kendall amused Hawke no end by fiercely telling the bartender that if he served her anything but fruit juice, she'd carry out the threat of days before.

With the curious probing of a new relationship, they pitted their skills against each other in various ways. He defeated her at tennis with a powerful serve and a devastating backhand. She won at poker, cheerfully telling him that she'd learned to play from her father while they were held as political prisoners in a foreign jail—a tale that quite probably destroyed Hawke's concentration.

He won at chess. She won at archery. He was better at skeet shooting, but when he set up a makeshift pistol range, he found Kendall to be the better shot.

Companionable. He teased her, cheerfully picking her up and carrying her whenever she stubbornly dug in her heels. He held her hand or put an arm around her waist constantly. He kissed her constantly—no matter where they were. Or who was watching.

And that was it. He escorted Kendall to her suite each evening, leaving her at the door with a kiss and an easy goodnight. He didn't try to come in. Didn't try to force her into anything.

By two A.M. on the third night Kendall had ruined three fingernails and had taken to muttering to herself. She was absolutely certain that Hawke was trying to drive her out of her mind. And she was every bit as sure that he was succeeding. Her sleep was fitful, her nerves raw. She felt as if he'd lit a fuse somewhere deep inside her, and she was going to explode any minute.

Pacing the floor of her sitting room with a vengeance, Kendall spared a rueful moment to consider Gypsy's defection.

Since Hawke had won her over, the cat had divided her nights between the two of them. Hawke hadn't complained; it seemed to amuse him. And since Gypsy had no trouble opening the connecting door, there wasn't much that Kendall could do about it. The cat was in his suite.

Sighing, Kendall kept pacing. The soft rustle of her long silk nightgown was the only sound in the room. She knew what Hawke was doing. He was leaving the decision up to her. And her body had been shrieking at her for the better part of a week to have done with the useless soul-searching and grab him with both hands.

But she was still afraid. Afraid of making a mistake. Afraid of being hurt. She had missed the teenage years of learning to test and trust relationships, the later years of learning what she wanted from relationships. Her emotional dependence on her father had cost her dearly; she saw that now.

She wanted Hawke. She loved him and wanted him. And she wanted to belong to him. But that was now. She didn't want to think about the future. That was the scary part.

As she paced, her eye was caught by the angel bell on the desk. Warily, she watched it as she paced to the balcony doors, then back to the hall door.

It's a magic bell, Kendall. When you ring it, it will always bring you a hawk.

It was absurd, of course. Utter nonsense. Fairy tale or not, she didn't believe in magic. She eyed the bell as she passed it again. He couldn't even *hear* it through the door. And he was probably already asleep anyway. Ridiculous.

And her imagination was playing tricks on her. The bell seemed to be whispering to her. She gave the desk a wide berth and paced to the balcony doors, staring out. She'd feel like a fool. And he would *not* come.

The next thing she knew, she was beside the desk. Detached, she watched her hand reach out steadily and pick up the little bell. It seemed to return her stare solemnly. "I'm not going to ring you," she whispered firmly. "It would be absurd."

She didn't ring the bell. She was certain of it. But there was a soft, delicate sound, like the music of elves. And the angel was smiling at her.

Carefully, Kendall placed the bell back on the desk and looked up. And he was there. The connecting door was closed; there had been no sound. He was looking at her gravely, questioningly. Darkly handsome in a deep blue robe. She watched him cross to her slowly, feeling her heart pounding madly. For once the sneering little voice inside her head was silent. This was right.

"Kendall?"

She couldn't respond, could only stare up at him, her need written on her face. With a soft, rough sound deep in his chest, Hawke swung her up into his arms and started for the bedroom.

Kendall stared into the gray eyes, telling him dreamily, "I didn't ring that bell, you know."

"Of course not." Hoarse though it was, his deep voice was amused.

"It rang itself." She smiled at him slowly. "Magic."

"Romance," he countered softly, lowering her gently onto the bed in the dimly lit room. His heavy weight immediately followed.

She welcomed him eagerly, thrusting her fingers through the thick dark hair and lifting her face invitingly for his kiss.

The past days had only heightened a desire that had been explosive from the very beginning, and Kendall gave herself up totally to that feeling. She was burning, on fire with sensations she had never known were possible. The touch of his mouth was like a brand, and she needed the searing pleasure of it.

She felt his tongue explore her mouth and met it with her own, her body shuddering in his arms. Her hands pushed the robe off his shoulders, and she was unaware when he threw it to the floor. His lips left hers at last, rough hands snapping the straps of her nightgown and slowly pushing the silky material down.

"Is this what you want?" he grated softly, his mouth hot on the sensitive flesh of her neck.

"Yes," she whispered. "Oh, yes . . ." She repeated his name over and over in her head, amazed to find that it sounded different. It sounded like a part of herself.

Hawke was slowly removing her gown, his mouth caressing bare skin an inch at a time. His lips toyed gently with first one nipple and then the other, his hands stroking, caressing. He seemed ravenous for the taste of her.

Kendall watched his absorbed face through half-closed eyes, her own hands exploring wonderingly the muscled strength of his back and shoulders. Her fingers clenched involuntarily on his shoulders when she felt his tongue dip hotly into her navel, and a soft moan escaped her trembling lips.

His caresses slid lower still, and she gasped, her senses going wild. She felt suspended, some instinct inside her waiting for something beyond her experience. Tension built within her like a coiled spring, a pleasure that was very nearly pain, and her body shuddered under the impact of it.

She was aching, empty, and she knew that only he could fill that emptiness, ease that pain. She shifted restlessly as he rose above her, her arms clinging around his neck. "Hawke . . ." she murmured huskily. "Hawke . . ."

He slid between her thighs, the gray eyes shot with silver as he stared down at her, his face taut. "Kendall," he rasped, his voice thick, impeded. "Take me and make me yours. . . ."

Kendall didn't wonder at the words. Not then. She was too caught up with what was happening between them. She felt him move suddenly, strongly, and her body arched involuntarily, her eyes widening with the primitive feeling of being *known,* fully and completely, for the first time in her life. It was a strange sensation, exciting and bewildering . . . and right.

She saw something flicker in the gray eyes as he went suddenly still, something startled and oddly fierce, and she wondered dimly if she should have warned him.

"Kendall?" he breathed.

She wound her arms tighter around his neck and pulled his head down, murmuring throatily against his lips, "Not *now!*"

With a soft groan his mouth clinging hungrily to hers, Hawke began to move. Instinct told her that he was keeping a tight rein on his passion, being gentle and careful and, though she loved him all the more for it, it wasn't gentleness that Kendall wanted.

Her body took fire in his arms, surrendering to him with yearning hunger and a demand of its own, a wild demand to have done with gentleness. Restraint dissolved, and Hawke took her as passionately as she offered herself, possessing her utterly.

And in that moment a bond was forged between them, stronger and deeper than either of them would realize for a long time. Forged in loving and needing, in knowledge and innocence, in a need so powerful that it swept all before it. They were tied together in the most basic way possible between a man and a woman. And nothing would ever be the same for either of them.

Drained, they rested in each other's arms, hearts gradually returning to normal. Kendall had never felt so wonderful, content to remain in his possessive embrace forever.

Hawke reached down to pull the covers up around them, then rose on an elbow to gaze at her with smoky eyes. "You've never been with a man before," he murmured wonderingly, his voice rough. "Why?"

Kendall felt suddenly amused, and soft laughter gleamed in her turquoise eyes. "You mean—why not? Or why now?"

He smiled crookedly. "Both."

She absently traced the scar on his chest. "Why not . . . because it never seemed to matter. Why now . . . because it does."

"Why does it matter now, honey?" he asked intensely.

"Because I—I need you." Her eyes shifted away from his in confusion, her own words jarring her oddly. Why did the simple statement make her feel suddenly dizzy?

"Well, that's something," he muttered in an odd voice. "And I guess something is better than nothing." Before she could respond, he went on lightly. "At least you rang the bell."

"I didn't," she objected immediately. "I swear it rang itself."

"Sure it did."

"Are you calling me a liar?"

"Yes."

Kendall giggled softly. "Well, I don't remember ringing it."

"You were in the throes of blinding passion, I expect," he told her gravely. "I think it's called amnesia."

She eyed him resignedly. "I think it's called malarkey."

"You *weren't* in the throes of blinding passion?" He sounded wounded.

"I didn't have amnesia."

"Ah—! An admission!"

Kendall flushed and glared at him. The man was enough to drive a saint to drink. "I wasn't in the throes of anything," she told him firmly, and then added with more dignity than accuracy, "I never let emotions rule my actions."

He started laughing. "Oh, really? And what about that little scene in the lobby a few days ago? Are you trying to tell me that your sweet little question was motivated by anything other than an emotional desire for revenge?"

"Of course," she said stoutly. "I just decided very logically that it was time to get even with you. Period."

"Uh-huh." Hawke lifted a quizzical brow. "Now explain why you rang the bell."

She stared at him, goaded. "I was out of my mind. Obviously."

"I resent that."

"Sorry."

Hawke grinned faintly. "You won't give an inch, will you? Why don't you just admit that you're crazy about me?"

Since the question was a light one, Kendall took it lightly. *"Crazy* is a good word for it. It's very difficult to keep one's sanity in the middle of a fairy tale. That tiara, for instance. Would you care to explain that to me?"

He accepted the change of subject without a blink. "I thought that the symbolism was obvious."

"That's not what I meant. Where did it come from, and why didn't you tell me that it was real?"

With a sigh Hawke answered, "It came from my namesake, and I didn't tell you it was real because I knew you'd never accept it."

She latched on to the first part of his answer. "The pirate? I thought so! Then it is an heirloom?"

"Who told you about the pirate?"

"Rick—when I asked him about the name of this island."

"Some friend. And, no, it isn't really an heirloom. In fact, it was probably stolen originally."

"Terrific. My crown is hot."

"Cute."

She sighed. "Well, really, Hawke—you shouldn't have given it to me. It belongs in your family, and—"

"And I wanted you to have it. Every fairy-tale princess deserves a crown, and now you've got one."

"This isn't a fairy tale!"

"You just admitted that it was. You said that it wasn't easy to keep your sanity in the middle of a fairy tale. Therefore—"

"Therefore, stop twisting my words! You know what I meant."

"No. Tell me."

Kendall frowned and tried to form her jumbled thoughts into some kind of reasonable order. "A fairy tale—isn't real. It has to end sooner or later. The story ends, the book is closed. It can't go on forever."

"Why not?" He smiled slightly. "Leave the book open, keep on writing the story. It doesn't have to end."

She gave him a frustrated look. "Hawke, I'm talking about *reality*. And storybook romance doesn't belong in a real world!"

As soon as the words left her mouth, Kendall was astonished by them. Was that why she was so afraid of the future? Did some tiny part of her mind stubbornly believe that what had happened between them couldn't be real and, therefore, couldn't last? Had she seen too much reality to believe in lovely dreams, to believe that romance could go on forever?

"Then we'll make our own world!" Hawke told her with sudden fierceness. He surrounded her face with warm hands, staring down at her intensely. "Kendall, don't you understand? I won't let the romance die."

"You can't keep it alive," she whispered, the child inside her finally understanding what happens when the book is closed. "The world closes in on you, and dreams are pushed aside."

"We'll close out the world."

"That's impossible."

"Is it?" He shook his head. "I don't think so. We've both seen too much of reality, honey. So we'll make our dream the reality."

She wanted to ask him how they could do that, but a wise little voice warned that the conversation was becoming too serious. If she didn't end it now, she would probably say something foolish and reckless. Deliberately keeping her voice light, she murmured, "Castles in the air."

Giving her a look of rueful understanding that was faintly unnerving, he followed her lead. "There's nothing wrong with that," he told her cheerfully. "As long as you build a firm foundation underneath."

"Out of what—clouds?"

The intensity was completely gone from his manner now as he laughed. "What else?"

Kendall thought vaguely that she had never met a man like him before. He seemed to have an uncanny ability to read her mind, to know when to push and when to back off. It was as if he were determined that she would make up her own mind. He had not said that he loved her or wanted to marry her, yet both had been implied in his words and actions.

He seemed almost to understand her confusion and uncertainty—even better than she did. And he seemed to feel—to *know*—that she would work it out herself, given time.

But Kendall wasn't so sure. Her love for him was too new, too fragile to put to the test. She was still afraid to take a chance. On him. On romance. And, most important, on herself.

Hawke laughed suddenly, looking down at her, his hands still warm on her face. "Do you realize this is the third time I've been in your bed?"

Her lips quirked involuntarily. "Well, they say the third time's the charm."

"I never thought I'd be grateful to an old adage."

Kendall found herself tracing the scar on his chest again. "You walked out on me the last time."

"You walked out on me first." His lips twisted. "Figuratively speaking, that is."

"That was your fault. If you'd warned me about that damned Purple Passion—"

"—I probably wouldn't have made it as far as your bed," he finished wryly.

"You make it sound like a race," she accused, laughing.

"Believe me, it's felt like a marathon. I'd very nearly decided to chain you to my bed and to hell with your psyche."

"Charming." She stared at him.

"I'm a charming guy."

Kendall choked. "What an ego!"

"I've never believed in hiding my light under a bushel."

"Any other interesting qualities I should know about?"

Hawke reflected for a moment. "I don't think so. Except one, maybe. It's only fair to warn you about that one."

"Which is?"

"Well, in addition to being charming, I'm also very determined. Very, very determined." He went on, his voice light and almost—but not quite—teasing. "And I always get what I want."

"Always?" When he nodded with a strange, glinting smile, Kendall felt extremely nervous.

"Always." He raked his fingers gently through her hair, gray eyes compelling as he stared down at her. "Struggle all you want, honey. Argue and protest, swear at me if you like. Find a thousand reasons to leave this island with your father."

It was what he *didn't* say that made Kendall swallow hard. She had seen his determination that very first day, and now she knew the full scope of it. "Hawke, I—"

"Not now." He lowered his head and kissed her almost playfully. "We can't spend all night talking."

Kendall wondered dimly what she had been about to say. She wasn't sure. "There isn't much of the night left," she told him now, beginning to feel dizzy and not particularly concerned with what tomorrow would bring.

"All the more reason not to waste it talking."

He kissed her again, not at all playfully this time, and

Kendall responded eagerly with a fire and demand to match his own.

She decided, quite suddenly, that she deserved this night with him. Every woman had the right—didn't she?—to spend one night with the man she loved. To love him freely and without reservation . . .

And let tomorrow take care of itself.

She wound her arms around his neck, shivering with pleasure when his tongue delicately probed the sensitive inner flesh of her lips. She could feel one of his hands still tangled in her hair, the other sliding warmly down her body. The covers were thrust away and she felt the cool air on her skin.

"I think," he muttered hoarsely, "that your eyes are lodestones. Turquoise lodestones. I can't get far away without being drawn back to them."

Her eyes opened and stared into the gray ones only inches away. With a need beyond reason, her fingers began slowly to explore his face. She felt his cheek tighten beneath her touch, but he was still, watching her. She moved her fingers over his face carefully, adding to the image already imprinted in her mind. And felt strangely moved when his lips quivered as she touched them softly.

"Kendall," he groaned almost soundlessly, abruptly burying his face in her throat. "I need you so much," he whispered against her soft, scented skin. "I need you to be a part of me."

She made a kittenlike sound of pleasure, holding his head

between her hands, twining her fingers in the thick darkness of his hair. Her skin felt incredibly sensitive, the slightest touch of his mouth sending her nerve endings into tingling delight. And she wondered dimly how she had lived twenty-five years without knowing these feelings were possible.

Before, they had both been driven by a passion held under restraint too long, but it was different this time. With the sharp edge of their hunger blunted, there was time to savor each moment, to explore and learn each other's bodies.

For a long time Kendall remained perfectly still beneath his touch. Rough hands traced the curves of her breasts, shaping and stroking the swelling mounds. His fingers tugged gently at the hard nipples, until his mouth took over, satisfying a hunger in both of them. Languidly, as though they had all the time in the world, his lips and tongue concentrated on the throbbing nipples.

Then his caresses moved lower, spreading tingling kisses on the sensitive flesh just beneath her breasts. His large hands spanned her tiny waist as he continued downward, his mouth sliding hotly over the flat belly and the sensitive skin below.

Kendall was breathing shallowly between barely parted lips, her concentration completely focused on him. His hands, his mouth, what he was doing to her. And then his mouth found the warm, womanly center of her, and an electric current raced through her.

"Hawke," she moaned, suddenly desperate to move, to

touch his body as he was touching hers. But he wouldn't allow it.

"Be still," he whispered roughly, the feel of his words on her flesh nearly driving her crazy. "Don't move . . . just feel . . ."

She tried to obey the deep command, closing her eyes and letting the feelings wash over her. She felt waves of heat moving outward from the core of her being, a curious icy heat. Tension built within her, coiling tighter and tighter. Desire went spinning into madness, and Kendall could no longer remain still.

She moved to his touch, breathing in rapid little pants, her need a living thing, desperate to escape. The feeling built to an impossible peak and she moaned deeply, her hands holding him until the knuckles went white. The world dissolved, and she was flying with wings that burned.

Kendall felt herself drifting for a timeless moment, and then the feeling subsided. Hawke moved back up her body to take her in his arms, his body tense against her damp flesh. He kissed her heated brow gently, pushing back a strand of silver-blond hair with fingers that weren't quite steady. Warm lips touched her closed eyes with butterfly softness.

She opened her eyes slowly, gazing up at him with the enigmatic mystery of a Siamese cat. The hunger in his eyes blazed with a silvery fire, and she felt her own need rise to meet it. Strength flowed back into her limbs, and she knew suddenly that she wanted more than anything to give him the same kind of pleasure he had given her.

With a strength and abandonment that surprised her, Kendall pushed against his chest until he rolled onto his back. She rose on his chest and then lowered her mouth to his, nibbling playfully on his lower lip, savoring the sweetness of their passion.

Feverishly, she explored his face and throat with her mouth, delighting in the clean, faintly salty taste of his skin. She tugged on his earlobe with her teeth, then flicked her tongue into the swirling inner ear, letting him feel her warm breath.

"Blow in my ear. . . ." The absurd jingle popped into her mind, and Kendall fought an insane desire to giggle. Her hell-bent humor . . . !

Thrusting the thought away, she let her lips trail down his neck until they reached his hair-rough chest. It rose and fell in time to his harsh breathing, and she spared a moment to look up and meet his eyes, her own darkened with desire.

"Witch," he grated softly, his hands shaping her shoulders and then sliding down her back. "Where did you learn this?"

"Ask my teacher," she murmured huskily, a particularly feminine little smile curving her lips.

Without waiting for a response, she dipped her head again, her lips searching for and finding the flat masculine nipples. She heard him groan softly and the sound spurred her on, a dizzying sense of power mounting to her head.

More than once in her life Kendall had been called upon to defend herself physically, and she had learned to do so quite skillfully. As she'd half seriously told Hawke, she knew several methods of causing pain, nasty little tricks picked up from several somewhat questionable acquaintances. But that ability to defeat someone twice her size had never given Kendall a feeling of power. That had been survival, pure and simple. But this . . .

This feeling of power, of having Hawke at her mercy, was strange and exciting. A brief illusion to be cherished for its brevity.

Glorying in the feeling, she caressed his nipples, using her tongue and teeth, and aware of an avid hunger she'd never known before. Her fingers tugged at the fine black hair on his chest, and then she moved lower, her mouth following the trail of hair arrowing down his flat stomach. She felt a heady need to explore every inch of his body, to know it as well as he knew hers.

Instinct guided her, curiosity fueled her desire. She had never known that a man's body could be so beautiful, and she went a little crazy in her attempt to imprint each strong characteristic on her mind and heart.

Her fingers trailed over his stomach and beyond, something inside of her dimly astonished at the soft, satiny feel of his skin. Gently now, she touched him, only half aware when he drew in his breath sharply, harshly. Just as she had concentrated before on what he had been doing to her, she concentrated now on what she was doing.

She bent her head suddenly, tasting his strength. She heard a groan rumble from deep in his chest, and that evidence of his pleasure increased her own. Knowledge came from somewhere, from deep in herself or from the desire to please him. She was completely uninhibited, no reluctance marring this experience for either of them.

The feeling of power remained, urging her on. She was in control, and that was a fascinating experience. In no other way could she control so completely, and the woman in her reveled in that.

"Kendall!" he rasped heavily, and then the room swung crazily and she found herself on her back, staring up at him. The gray eyes contained a hot glitter. "Witch . . . beautiful witch. God, you're driving me out of my mind!"

There was no gentleness in his kisses then, only driving need and a hunger that rose in a flaming fury to meet her own. Kendall clung to him eagerly, branding him with her mouth, her nails unconsciously digging into his back. She felt him move strongly and welcomed him, her body arching against his, beneath the weight that trapped and possessed.

Kendall felt herself rise to meet him, impatient, driven. She held him with all of her body, using muscles she'd been unaware of until then, and saw the surprise and sudden flickering excitement in his eyes. His face was hard and taut, the lamplight casting shadows and highlights, and Kendall wondered dizzily if there would ever be enough time to know his face in all its expressions.

Together, they moved in a graceful rhythm, as if each were a part of the other. Time vanished . . . or stood still . . . or had never existed. Only the two of them and this piercing, spiraling excitement existed. Like a runaway ocean wave, it swept them up and carried them along in a fierce rush.

Kendall moaned raggedly when the wave reached its peak, calling out his name mindlessly and hearing her own name torn from his throat with a shuddering groan.

And then the wave burst on the shore, leaving them spent and very nearly numb, damp bodies tangled together.

The air-conditioned room felt almost cold to her heated body, but Kendall felt too pleasantly exhausted to move. As a matter of fact, if somebody had yelled fire, she wouldn't even have opened her eyes. Apparently, Hawke felt the same.

Stirring slightly beside her, Hawke murmured, "Do you always sleep in an icebox?"

"It's your hotel," she pointed out, rousing herself enough to snuggle closer to him.

"It's your room. What's the thermostat set on?"

"What strange things you find to talk about . . . and at

such strange moments." She sighed sleepily. "I don't know what the thermostat's set on."

"I like my creature comforts. And it's like the fringes of Siberia in here." He began to run his fingers through her hair. "You're better than a cat though."

"I beg your pardon?"

He chuckled softly. "Well, your cat's been sharing my bed, you know. Almost as good as an electric blanket. But you're better."

"Gee, thanks."

"You're welcome." He raised his head suddenly, looking down toward the foot of the bed. "Hell. No wonder I'm freezing. What did you do with the covers, you brazen hussy?"

Kendall giggled, nuzzling her face into his neck. "I didn't do anything with them. An impatient male foot kicked them away."

"Liar."

"I swear."

"I don't remember that."

With another sleepy giggle, she told him, "I'm not surprised. You had other things on your mind. It's really very flattering. To me, I mean."

"Get the covers."

"Get them yourself."

Hawke sighed. "Didn't you hear the voice of your lord and master?"

"Lincoln freed the slaves."

"You're going to let me freeze on a technicality?"

"No, you'll freeze on a bed."

"Cute. That's cute."

Kendall delicately bit the side of his neck. "It'll teach you not to make dumb conversation with a woman you just seduced."

"*I* seduced? Who rang the bell?"

"What bell?"

Hawke released a sighing laugh. "Are you going to get the covers?"

"No."

"You should be whipped."

"Feeling energetic?"

He chuckled softly and managed somehow to pull the covers up around them without dislodging Kendall. "Maybe later."

"I can hardly wait." She smothered a yawn against his neck, feeling herself drift and letting sleep come.

C h a p t e r

9

When the phone began ringing early the next morning, Kendall's first thought was a disgusted *I can never sleep late in this damn place!* Eyes firmly shut, she reached out a hand and fumbled on the nightstand for the phone. Lifting the receiver, she suddenly became aware of an unaccustomed weight across her waist.

Still holding the receiver inches from her ear, she opened one eye and stared at the male arm lying possessively over her stomach. Kendall opened the other eye and turned her head slowly, gazing at Hawke's relaxed, sleeping face.

Absently, she brought the phone to her ear, murmuring, "Hello?" in a bemused voice.

"Kendall?" It was Rick, obviously hesitant and more than a little embarrassed. "I'm sorry for disturbing you so early, but —uh—you wouldn't happen to know where Hawke is, would you?"

She felt an absurd desire to giggle, and hastily choked it back. Oh, well. The hotel staff and guests already considered her a fallen woman. This only confirmed it. Sighing, she said ruefully, "Hang on a minute, Rick."

"Sure." There was a definite laugh in his voice.

Kendall covered the mouthpiece with her fingers and poked her companion gently with an elbow. "Hawke? *Hawke* —wake up."

Gray eyes opened with obvious reluctance and stared at her sleepily. There was a puzzled expression at first, and then a sudden light flared deep in the smoky depths. "Good morning," he said huskily. Apparently, he didn't notice the phone.

"Good morning." She smiled as he rose on an elbow to stare down at her, his arm tightening across her middle. He bent his head, kissing her gently.

Kendall lifted her free hand to touch his cheek lightly, feeling his morning beard scratch her fingers sensuously.

"What time is it?" he asked.

"I don't know. Dawn, I think."

A purely male grin tugged at his lips. "Just couldn't wait any longer, huh?"

"Right." She prodded the middle of his chest with the phone. "But first—you have a call. Rick."

"Oh." He looked absurdly disappointed. "Hell. What does he want?"

"I didn't ask," Kendall told him politely.

Hawke sighed and took the receiver from her. "What is it, Rick? And it damn well better be important, or I'll send you back to Florida the hard way." His voice wasn't very clear, because he was pressing tiny kisses against Kendall's fingers one at a time.

She watched him, still bemused, thinking how nice it was to wake up beside the man she loved, to see his eyes light up when he saw her. She tuned out the conversation between Hawke and his manager, just staring at his face and feeling very alive and very awake in spite of her lack of sleep.

Hawke hung up the phone finally, resting a bit more of his weight on her as he leaned over to reach the nightstand. Without bothering to prop himself back up, he stared down at her wryly. "I guess you heard."

Kendall blinked at him. "No. I . . . wasn't listening."

He smiled crookedly. "As much as I hate it—and you'll never know how much I hate it—I'm afraid I'll have to leave you. There's a domestic crisis going on in the kitchen, and Rick claims he can't handle it." Hawke reflected for a moment. "And if I find out that he could have handled it, I just may kill him."

Her lips twitched. "And lose a good manager? You wouldn't."

"I'd rather have you than that bum any day."

"How flattering."

Hawke grinned. "One of these days," he said ruefully,

"you're going to realize that I never say anything I don't mean. You seem determined to take everything I say as a joke."

"It's safer that way," she told him solemnly.

"There you go again." He shook his head despairingly. "What do I have to do to convince you I'm serious?"

"Well, you might look a little more dignified with your clothes on."

He lifted a quizzical brow. "But naked people have very few secrets. Wouldn't you agree?"

"And very little dignity."

Firmly, he told her, "The world would be much better off if we all went naked."

"Very sunburned too."

"Dammit, will you be serious for just a minute!"

Kendall eyed him consideringly. "You mean you really think we should all go naked? I'm not sure that's a rational fantasy."

"Rational fantasy is a contradiction in terms."

"Thank you, Professor Madison."

Hawke dropped his head suddenly, burying his face between her breasts. "Oh, God," he groaned, "how do we get into these ridiculous conversations?"

Kendall raked her fingers through his dark hair and giggled in spite of herself. "It must be lack of sleep. Or exhaustion." She felt giddy and happy, and didn't want to think about anything important.

It was amazing to her that she felt so comfortable lying in bed with a man she'd known for an embarrassingly short time. She thought back suddenly to the deal they'd made the first night, and realized that Hawke had kept his end of it. He hadn't forced her into anything. And not once had she been forced to say no to him. In fact, she'd never even wanted to.

He was sighing against her flesh. "I'll go along with that," he said in a muffled voice. "And I could shoot Rick for waking us up."

"Speaking of Rick—"

"I know." He lifted his head, gazing down at her with restless eyes. "But I don't want to leave you. I have this awful feeling that I dreamed last night."

The wry statement touched Kendall oddly, and she raised her head from the pillow to kiss him lightly. "Just how important is that crisis?" she murmured invitingly.

"Very, if we want to eat." The words were light, but his gray eyes had taken on a look she recognized from the previous night. "The cook's threatening to quit. He's French, and very excitable."

"All the best ones are," she said.

Hawke groaned and abruptly rolled away from her. "I'm getting out of here before we get into another one of those absurd conversations. God only knows where we'd end up this time!"

Kendall laughed and watched him, absently drawing the covers up over her breasts.

"Where's my robe? I could have sworn—"

"It's on the floor. There, by the—" She choked suddenly and began to laugh. For the very first time, she got a good look at his scar. It was on his hip, just below the tanned line indicating where he wore his bathing suit. He'd have to back up to a mirror to see it clearly himself.

A very neat, even, double row of teeth marks.

No wonder her question had embarrassed him! Kendall couldn't stop laughing, and Hawke's wry expression wasn't helping any.

He pulled on his robe and tied the belt securely. "I don't see what's so funny," he muttered, obviously lying.

"Hawke—" She finally managed to get control of herself. "How did you get that scar? Or is that a dumb question?"

"How I got it is obvious."

Kendall made an effort to straighten out her face. "Did you make somebody mad at you?" she asked innocently.

He sank down on the foot of the bed and dropped his head into his hands. "You're going to be the death of me," he groaned.

"Hawke—*what happened?*"

He raised his head and stared at her, a faint tinge of red creeping up his lean cheeks. "I don't remember," he told her flatly.

"What? Come on, now!"

"I swear." He sighed and gestured to the tattoo on his forearm. "It happened the same night I got this. That's all I know."

"The night your buddies got you drunk?" When he nodded, Kendall said gravely, "So you woke up the next morning with a terrific hangover, lying on silken cushions in Madame Wong's Whoopie Parlor?"

He gave her a startled look. "There weren't any silken cushions," he muttered, tacitly admitting the rest.

Biting the inside of her lip to keep from bursting out laughing again, she asked, "Wasn't Rick one of those buddies? Can't he tell you what happened that night?"

"Judging by the way he snickers from time to time," Hawke said disgustedly, "I'm sure he could. But he won't. He's kept that damn story to himself for nearly fifteen years. I've tried threats, pleading, bribery—nothing works. I'll go to my grave wondering."

Before Kendall could respond, the phone rang demandingly, and she reached for the receiver. "He's coming, Rick," she said cheerfully into the mouthpiece.

"Well, tell him to hurry, will you?" The manager sounded harassed, angry voices rising in the background. "With all due respect to your love life, we have to eat—and Jean's packing his suitcase!"

Kendall winced as a crash of china erupted from Rick's

end, then hung up the phone with a laugh when the line went dead. "Jean's packing," she informed Hawke. "And somebody's throwing dishes around. You'd better get down there."

Hawke sighed and got to his feet. He looked down at her for a moment, and Kendall could have sworn that his face was a bit strained. Lightly, he said, "I hope you're not planning to catch the first banana boat out of here the moment my back's turned."

She reached behind her head to plump up her pillow, murmuring evasively, "I promised my father that I'd wait here for him."

Something flickered in Hawke's eyes and then was gone. "So I have that much time."

"To do what?" Kendall wasn't sure she wanted an answer, but Hawke gave her one.

"Convince you to stay here. I was hoping that last night had done that, but I see I was wrong. You're still running, aren't you, honey?"

"I don't know what you mean."

"Yes, you do. You're not hiding behind that dumb-blonde act anymore, but you're still running. You're scared stiff of committing yourself, afraid of being hurt. So you're running from me, from yourself, and from what we feel."

Kendall felt a flicker of resentment. He was ruining things by injecting reality into last night's dream, and she didn't want to think about that. "You'd better go take care of your crisis."

He took a step closer to her side and stared down at her unreadable expression. Then, with a certain deliberation, he said casually, "Just remember—you've got responsibilities now." He bent down and patted her blanket-covered belly lightly, briefly. "There may well be a little bird in the nest right now." He turned and left the room before he could see her shock.

Kendall stared after him, his careless words bringing home to her the enormity of what she had done.

A baby?

She closed her eyes tightly, seeing in her mind the thousands of children she had met all over the world. Children she had loved—however briefly. She wanted a child of her own, a child who would never know hunger or cold. A child who would never dance laughingly over a mine in the middle of a war . . .

A dark-haired boy with gray eyes. Or a little girl with her father's smile. A houseful of kids, surrounded by love and laughter.

Shoving the image fiercely from her mind, Kendall pulled herself from the bed and headed for the shower. It was highly unlikely that she could be pregnant after one night. Highly unlikely. Hawke had no right to imply that she could be, just to upset her.

But had that been his intention? Somehow, she didn't think so. There had been a satisfied gleam in his gray eyes, that gleam that she'd already learned to be wary of. He had left that thought in her mind deliberately.

Kendall took her shower, allowing herself to dream a bit about an unborn child that might never be. She washed her hair, then got out and dried herself with a fluffy towel before going into her bedroom to find her hair dryer.

Half an hour later she was dressed in shorts and a knit pullover and, after checking Gypsy's food and water dishes and thinking wryly that at least her cat was sleeping late, left her suite. She needed to think, and pacing around in her room wasn't going to help her do that. Maybe fresh air would.

It was very early; none of the guests seemed to be up and about. The lobby was deserted except for Rick, who was behind the desk, on the phone, and looking as harassed as he'd sounded earlier. And from the looks of his rumpled blond hair, he'd been clutching it in despair.

Kendall leaned against the desk and watched him, unabashedly listening to his end of the conversation. Apparently, it was from the other hotel, which seemed to be having a domestic crisis of its own. Rick was trying to explain that Hawke wasn't available at the moment, and obviously wasn't getting through to the party on the other end of the line. He finally hung up the phone with a faint bang and glared across the desk at Kendall.

"Job getting you down?" she inquired with mock sympathy.

The glare contained a faintly desperate, despairing glitter. "Why don't you and Hawke just feed me to the sharks and be done with it?" he demanded irritably. "He's ready to cut my throat with a blunt knife for disturbing you two; God only knows what he'll do when he finds out that his other manager's about to walk out because he can't deal with *his* cook either. Go ahead—feed me to the sharks! I'd welcome peaceful oblivion."

Kendall widened her eyes innocently. "Did I say anything?"

"I read minds," he muttered. "It's a new ability, acquired out of sheer desperation. Is it *my* fault that this just happens to be one of those days when everything goes wrong? Is it *my* fault that Jean decided to decorate the kitchen with broken china? Is it *my* fault that I can't speak French, and didn't understand a word he was screaming?"

"Of course not," Kendall murmured soothingly.

Rick leaned an elbow on the desk and propped his chin in his hand. Sighing, he said wryly, "So put in a good word for me with Hawke, will you? I'll apologize on bended knees if it'll help."

She looked amused. "For everything going wrong?"

"No. For disturbing you two."

At this point Kendall was beyond being embarrassed by anything. She smiled sweetly at Rick. "I know a way you can make it up to both of us."

"Anything."

"Tell me how Hawke got that scar."

"Anything except that." Rick grinned suddenly. "I love to watch his face when I chuckle over that story."

"Hawke called it a snicker."

"He would."

Kendall sighed. "I hope he fires you. But first, we'll boil you in oil. It's cruel not to tell him."

Rick looked at her with bright, laughing eyes. "Of course it is. And it was cruel of you to keep the poor guy on tenterhooks all this week. I assume everything's settled now?"

She gave him a puzzled look. "Everything?" A flush rose in her face in spite of all her efforts, and she shrugged. "There's nothing to settle."

His grin faded. "I'm sorry, Kendall," he said hesitantly. "I didn't mean to pry. It's just that the entire hotel—myself included—has been watching the romance. I know it can't have been easy for you, being courted in a goldfish bowl. But I was hoping things had worked out for you two." He paused for a moment, then added softly, "Because you love him."

Kendall stared at him for a moment, then squared her shoulders. "I need some air," she muttered revealingly. Without another word to him she turned and left the lobby.

She moved through the deserted dining room and out to the terrace, where tables were placed for anyone who wanted to eat outside. All the tables were vacant now, and Kendall walked past them to lean against the railing absently.

Rick's comments had shaken her oddly, particularly the last one. If he had seen how she felt, then who else had? Did Hawke know? She didn't think so. At least, he couldn't be sure how she felt. Just as she couldn't be sure about his feelings.

Kendall stared blindly out toward the ocean, not seeing, now, the view she had admired so often. Vaguely, she wondered exactly what Hawke wanted from her. He wanted her to stay, she knew, but for how long? As mistress or wife? Was he still digging for those secrets he'd seen that first day . . . or had his determined digging uncovered them all?

He'd said once that he wanted to take care of her, to protect her from pain. To spoil her and bring her flowers and silly presents. To surround her with beauty and romance, and make sure that she never had nightmares.

From any other man, she would have considered that a declaration of love. But from Hawke, she wasn't sure. *Was* it all just an elaborate game to him? A determined campaign launched because of some obscure reason? Sex? No . . . that couldn't be it. Unless he wanted more than one night. Because he still wanted her to stay.

The romantic "courtship," the gifts and whimsical conversation, all pointed to love. But if that was the case, why hadn't he told her that he loved her? It just didn't make sense. He had to know that she would be wary of committing herself without some assurance from him.

Or was that the reason? Did he want her to commit herself with no certainty of his feelings? God . . . what a chance she'd be taking! Gambling her life on the chance that he loved her, or could learn to love her. Making herself totally and completely vulnerable to him, and leaving herself wide open to possible heartache. And if he rejected her, or tired of her at some future date . . . it didn't bear thinking of.

Because Kendall knew, with a sudden hollow certainty, that she would never love another man this way. Her father had once told her that her ancestors had been known for having only one great love in their lives. Curious, she had traced back several hundred years and found that, apparently, to be the truth. Husbands or wives had died, but there had been no second marriages. Not even for reasons common in the past: securing an heir, or a son to work the fields, or making an advantageous marriage to increase the family holdings.

And her own father had been devastated when his beloved Jenny had died. He would not remarry.

Loving was, almost by definition, taking a chance. On small things. Did he like sleeping with the window open while you froze to death? Could he bear the old movies you were addicted to? Could you bear his football games? Who would take out the garbage? Little things, generally worked out by compromise.

And then there were the big chances, the ones you had no control over. What if love died? What if he had a dangerous job, or loved racing dangerous cars as a hobby? What if you lost him?

Kendall began to realize then just how little she knew about human relationships. And about trust. In spite of her love for Hawke, she was afraid to trust him. With a single sneering word he could destroy her, and even though she didn't believe him capable of such cruelty, the very possibility terrified her.

And what if the love she felt wasn't love at all? On the heels of her decision to let go of her father, she had fallen in love. Or had she? Had she simply transferred her feelings from one to the other? No.

No. She loved Hawke, and she still loved her father. Two totally different kinds of love. But there was another fear eating at her.

What if her love made her cling too closely to him? She could lose herself, she could—*No, stop it!* she scolded the Cassandra voice in her head sharply.

Kendall was a strong woman, and she knew it. She was afraid of committing herself, just as anyone would fear the unknown. But, God knew, she had faced worse fears. She hadn't exactly been thrilled about jumping out of that plane years before, but the alternative had been more frightening. And she could distinctly remember facing a man more than twice her size, with ugliness in his eyes. She'd fought—and won—because the alternative was unthinkable.

Was that courage? She didn't know. At the time it had been simple survival. A choice of alternatives.

And what was her alternative now? She could love Hawke, taking the chance that he wouldn't hurt her. Swallow her fear and her pride, and accept whatever he could give her, without asking for or expecting more. Or she could leave.

Before Kendall could consider what that would mean, she heard a step behind her on the terrace. And she knew who it was. Making her voice light, she asked, "Is Jean all smoothed down?"

"God, I hope so." Hawke slid his arms around her waist from behind, drawing her back against him. He rubbed his chin lightly in her hair. "Ummm . . . you smell terrific."

"Thank you." She smiled slightly, still gazing out to sea. "It must be the herbal shampoo."

He laughed softly, ruefully. "You have no romance in your soul."

"I know. It's sad, isn't it?"

"Extremely. I don't know what I'm going to do with you."

"I'm undersized too. You could throw me back."

His arms tightened, and Kendall could have sworn she felt tension creep into his lean frame. "Does that mean I've caught you?" he asked lightly.

She felt her heart begin to thud, and hoped he couldn't

feel it. Or hear it. "Don't be ridiculous," she managed to say with mocking dignity. "I'm not a fish."

He sighed softly. "There you go again. Just when I think I've got you backed into a corner, you always manage to slip away. Do you like playing games?"

"Do you?" The question was out before she could halt it, and Kendall bit her lip when he remained silent for a moment. She felt one of his hands move away, and then he was quickly, deftly placing a necklace around her neck.

"Present for you."

She looked down for a moment, then lifted the small medallion and stared at it. It was beautiful, delicate, made of fine gold, and obviously very old. A hawk in flight.

Quietly, she told him, "You shouldn't keep giving me presents."

"I haven't given you a gift in days." He sounded wounded. "It cut me to the quick too, but you were getting upset with me, so I stopped."

"It's beautiful. Thank you." Her voice was unusually meek —almost toneless.

"Kendall—"

Quickly, she said, "You have to go to the other hotel, don't you? I—I think I'll go for a walk on the beach."

"Later." Firmly, he grasped her shoulders and turned her around to face him. Lifting her chin with one hand, he stared down into the curiously blank turquoise eyes. His jaw tightened. "Dammit—you're thinking about leaving me!"

She blinked. "Just a walk. I—"

His hand dropped back to her shoulder and he shook her slightly. "To hell with the walk! I won't let you dodge the subject this time. Is that your answer to everything, Kendall? Running away?"

She had never seen him so angry, a muscle leaping violently in his jaw and the gray eyes blazing. And her own temper surged to the surface. "That's not fair," she declared tightly, pushing his hands away and stepping back.

"Isn't it? All I have to do is hint at some kind of commitment, and you shy away like a scared rabbit!"

"Is that surprising?" She glared at him, feeling raw-nerved and oddly unlike herself. "You're practically a stranger!"

His face hardened. "You can say that now? After last night? What did that mean to you, Kendall—just another game?"

"You started the games," she accused him unevenly. "You're the one who started playing at being a knight!"

"And it looks like I've been tilting at windmills, doesn't it?" His voice was strangely harsh.

Kendall felt her anger drain away, leaving only confusion and uncertainty behind it. Almost whispering, she told him, "Storybook romance doesn't belong in a real world."

"Then where does it belong, Kendall?" His voice was still

rough. "Between the covers of a child's book? Is it something we outgrow and then push aside, saying, To hell with it? You tell me where it says that romance is wrong!"

She stared at him, wishing that she knew the right answers, wishing that he would take her to bed and make love to her until she forgot all the questions.

Hawke stepped closer, reaching out to cup her face with warm hands, his face softening abruptly as though he could see or sense her confusion. "Stay with me," he said quietly, almost pleadingly. "Let me take care of you. Let me show you that romance does belong in a real world."

Unsteadily, she told him, "Emotionally . . . I've only just stopped clinging to my father. And now you want me to turn right around and cling to you?"

"Kendall, it isn't *clinging!*" His gray eyes moved restlessly over her face. "It's *sharing.* Sharing laughter and love—*and* storybook romance, dammit!"

Her heart jumped at the word "love" and she swallowed hard. "It's happening too fast . . . I can't think. You don't understand!"

"I understand," he told her softly. "I understand that you're afraid—and that's normal. And I understand that you're thinking of running away—and that's not."

Kendall backed away from him slowly, suddenly desperate to get away somewhere and think. She couldn't think when he stared at her that way, with that strange intensity.

"Kendall?"

"I'm going for a walk," she said almost inaudibly.

His face tightened again. "Just don't run," he grated out softly.

She very nearly did, turning quickly and hurrying down the steps and toward the path leading to the beach. He didn't follow her. But then—she hadn't expected him to.

She walked slowly up the beach, heading inland when she reached the cliffs and then wandering without realizing toward the village. Her thoughts were jumbled for a long time; nothing made sense to her.

Did Hawke love her? She thought that perhaps he did, but why hadn't he said so? From deep inside her came a quiet little voice, offering a possible answer. *Maybe he was afraid too.* Oh, God—such a little word to tie grown people into knots!

Was he afraid of leaving himself completely vulnerable to her, just as she was afraid? Did he, too, wonder what would happen when the commitment was made and tomorrow opened its doors?

Questions. Endless questions. All boiling down to a final, inescapable one. One she had to face. One she had to answer. Did she love him enough to risk everything on that love?

If she left him and his island, she wouldn't be alive anymore. Oh, she'd probably go on existing. Walking, talking, eating, maybe even laughing from time to time. But she wouldn't be alive.

She thought of last night, and felt an intense pain at the possibility of never knowing that kind of sharing again. She couldn't give that up. And she couldn't give up the laughter and the teasing. She couldn't give up . . . him.

Only a few days, a short span of time, and she was tied to him. He was the friend she had always wanted. The lover who had taken her on a journey to a wondrous, enchanted land. Where there were castles and crowns and unicorns. Where dreams were alive.

"I—need you." She heard her voice saying words that had jarred her at the time, although she hadn't known why. And then she heard his voice, whispering huskily, *"I need you to be a part of me."*

Kendall stopped walking suddenly, only half aware that she was on the sidewalk in the village.

And suddenly she had the answer. She needed him. It was that simple. She needed him to make her whole, complete. He was the half of herself she hadn't known was missing.

And wasn't that worth taking a chance on?

He could hurt her. He could, in fact, destroy her. But she would destroy herself if she didn't take this chance. For the rest of her life what-might-have-been would eat at her like a cancer. Even supposing that she could turn and walk away from him . . . and Kendall knew that she couldn't. It would be walking away from her very soul.

She thought of romance. Of a man who could unabashedly court a woman in a crowded lobby or on a deserted beach. And a woman who told that man foolishly that romance wasn't real.

Kendall looked down at the lovely medallion, lifting it in fingers that weren't steady. Gently, she turned it, watching the light reflect off it in a warm glow. And then the inscription on the back, tiny though it was, leapt out at her. It was a new inscription, she knew, the letters bright gold from a jeweler's tool. And it was an old Arab proverb she recognized.

THERE ARE THREE THINGS THAT CAN NEVER BE HIDDEN: A MOUNTAIN, ONE RIDING A CAMEL, AND THE FACE OF A MAN IN LOVE.

She felt absurd tears start to her eyes. Oh, God—how stupid she was! The man had done everything but crawl to her on his knees, and she just wouldn't let herself believe!

It wasn't a game to him any more than it was to her. She was in love with an honest-to-God romantic man. And there was an almost delirious joy in that.

Kendall blinked at the surrounding scenery as she realized abruptly where she was. She started to turn toward the direction of the hotel, impatient, all at once, to run to Hawke and tell him how stupid she'd been. But then her eyes focused on the window display of the shop she was standing in front of.

In the center of the display was a necklace lying over a black velvet stand. It was obviously a man's necklace. Intricately braided leather held a medallion unlike any she had ever seen before. It was carved from the finest milky opal, containing tiny points of pink and green in its depths. A delicate mythical creature, symbolizing innocence and purity. Her symbol. A unicorn.

Kendall stared at the beautiful creature for a moment, then looked down at the hawk in her hand. Her gaze rose again to the unicorn. Perfect. It would be perfect. If only . . .

Would the shopkeeper send the bill to the hotel? Of course he would! Today was her day.

C h a p t e r 10

Kendall hurried through the glass doors, waving a distracted hello to Max and not giving him the time to open them for her. She slowed her pace once she was inside, her eyes searching the crowded lobby for Hawke. If only he hadn't yet gone to the other hotel, or hadn't had to go. . . . She didn't want to waste another minute.

He was lounging against the side of the desk, talking casually to Rick, looking around when Rick saw her. Gray eyes unreadable, he watched her slow walk across the lobby.

Kendall halted about ten feet away and stared at him for a moment, then abruptly threw the unicorn necklace at him. He caught it easily, looked down at it for a moment, then straightened and casually placed it around his neck. Then he waited.

She was only dimly aware of the crowded lobby, some portion of her mind noting that the guests were all waiting, just as Hawke was, for the final chapter in this peculiar courtship.

She wet her lips nervously and murmured, "If I have to wear your symbol, the least you can do is wear mine." Still, he waited. "I—I love you," she ventured hesitantly.

A muscle leapt in his lean jaw, and something flickered in the gray eyes; other than that, he gave no sign that her confession had moved him. "And now?" he asked gruffly.

Kendall's mind flew back to the evening he had found her on the cliffs and she had talked briefly about her life. He had asked that question then, the same question she had asked herself as she wondered what she wanted to do with her life. She hadn't been able to answer it then.

And her hell-bent sense of humor surfaced abruptly as she understood what he wanted to hear. "You're going to make me say it, aren't you?"

He nodded slowly, still watching her.

Kendall thought of the several things she'd like to do with him. Feed him to the sharks. Strangle him with the necklace. Stab him with one of his damned monogramed forks. Imprison him in her bed.

The last one won out.

She squared her shoulders and met the unreadable gaze bravely. "Will you marry me?"

The tension she hadn't noticed until then drained suddenly from his face, and he took a deep, shuddering breath. "Hell," he grated, striding toward her, "I thought you'd never ask!"

And even through the haze of her own raging emotions, Kendall distinctly heard the crowd in the lobby heave a collective sigh of relief. Or was it envy?

She threw her arms around his neck as he reached her, raising a glowing face for his kiss. And Hawke met her lips with a fierce hunger and possessiveness. He swept her up into his arms and carried her to the elevator, apparently deciding that audiences were fine—up to a point.

Staring at Hawke's face, Kendall vaguely heard Amanda Foster addressing someone in the lobby. "I'm *so* glad I decided to stay another week," she was saying happily. "I just had to know how the romance turned out!"

Kendall giggled softly as Hawke stepped into the elevator, and asked him gravely, "Is the romance over?"

"Never," he vowed softly, staring down at her face with burning silvery eyes. "It's only just begun, darling."

Kendall sighed happily and tightened her arms around his neck, impatient to get up to her room or his. Wherever. But she felt duty-bound to voice a protest. "What about the problems at the other hotel? Rick said—"

"I've already taken care of it. If anything else comes up, Rick can handle it." He smiled at her slowly. "You and I have other plans."

"Oh, really?" Kendall could hear the breathlessness in her voice. "What have you got in mind?"

The elevator doors opened, and Hawke began striding

down the hall. "An entire day. Just the two of us, all alone in my room. We'll lock the door, hang out the Do Not Disturb sign, and take the phone off the hook."

"And then?" she asked innocently.

Hawke grinned, bending down to open the unlocked door of his suite and kicking it closed behind them. "Do you really have to ask—after last night?"

He set her on her feet just inside the sitting room, keeping his arms around her. Kissing her tenderly, he muttered, "God, Kendall—I was afraid you were going to run away from me!"

Kendall stood on tiptoe to fit her body more firmly against the hard length of his, her fingers smoothing the dark hair at his nape. "I could never have done that," she whispered. "No matter how scared I was of committing myself, the thought of leaving you was even more terrifying. I love you, Hawke—I want to spend the rest of my life with you."

"I don't think that will be long enough," he told her thickly. "Eternity won't be long enough. I love you so much, honey—I'll never be able to tell you how much."

In spite of knowing, deep inside her, that Hawke loved her, she still felt a sense of wonder at hearing the words. "You love me? Really love me?"

He smiled a little wryly, but the gray eyes were looking at her with much the same wonder. "Why do you think I've been chasing after you like a man demented ever since you walked through the doors? I've loved you from the very beginning."

"When did you know?" she asked huskily.

"That first day, after you pulled Robbie from the pool. I told you that Robbie was an orphan, and you were staring off into space, that hurting look in your eyes. I wanted to wipe the expression away, to make sure no one ever hurt you again." His arms tightened around her. "What about you? When did that stubborn little heart of yours finally cave in?"

"I have a sneaking suspicion that I was falling all along." She smiled ruefully. "But I didn't really admit it to myself until the night you walked out on me."

"That long ago?" He frowned fiercely. "Why didn't you tell me?"

"Are you kidding? You were being a perfect gentleman those next few days. Almost brotherly, in fact. Leaving me at my door every night. What were you trying to do—break my spirit?"

His frown turned into a grin. "So that started getting to you, huh? I was hoping it would."

"Beast."

"But lovable."

"True." Kendall stared up at him curiously. "Tell me something. Did you really hear the bell?"

He chuckled softly. "Of course. Honey, I had my ear to that damned door every night!"

She started laughing. "Romance!"

"Of course. And that's what threw you off balance, wasn't it? You thought I was playing some kind of game."

"Well, you can't really blame me! There I was, being outrageously courted by a man I'd just met. A man who had this strange habit of picking me up and carrying me, giving me sometimes puzzling gifts, making love to me in elevators, and embarrassing me in front of people. It's a wonder I didn't feed you to the flytrap!"

Hawke gave her a quizzical look. "You're the one who finally gave in under the eyes of half the hotel guests."

"It seemed appropriate," she murmured.

Reproachfully, he told her, "And you threw the necklace at me. The first gift you'd ever given me, and you threw it like a hand grenade!"

Kendall grinned slightly. "That seemed appropriate too!" She hesitated for a moment, then said slowly, "We both know why I didn't admit how I felt, but what about you? You never once said that you loved me."

"Because I thought you'd run like hell. Every time I even hinted at commitment, you changed the subject in a second. I was going crazy trying to think of some way to keep you here long enough to convince you I wasn't playing games."

He looked at her wryly. "You were the only one who didn't know. My mother knew after a single phone call, and Rick's been giving me silly grins every time he sees me."

Kendall sighed. "Well, they knew how I felt too. Why were we the last ones to find out?"

"You were stubborn."

"I resent that."

Hawk smiled, but said huskily, "I was going to tell you how I felt this morning. I'd felt hopeful after last night. So I decided to tell you that I loved you, and try to convince you that I meant it. But then Rick called, and you were being evasive again."

"I'm sorry, darling," Kendall whispered, reaching up to kiss him lightly.

His eyes flared. "Do you realize," he said thickly, "that you've never called me that before?"

Kendall tilted her head to one side, considering. "I think I like the sound of it."

"So do I. It's something I'll never grow tired of hearing." His arms tightened around her and he bent his head, nuzzling the side of her neck. "Or saying. I love you, darling. You're the beautiful love I'd given up all hope of finding."

Kendall held his face between her hands when he raised his head, looking up at him with glowing eyes. "And you're the love I didn't believe in, the dream I thought I'd outgrown. The other half of myself. Oh, Hawke, I love you so much! How did I ever exist without you?"

He kissed her gently, and then passion arced between them like a live spark. Kendall clung to him, returning the kiss feverishly, her fingers locked in his hair. She could feel the need in him, the matching need in herself, and gave herself up totally to the joy of this moment.

Hawke lifted his head at last, breathing roughly, silver fire in his eyes. But before he could say anything, a slight sound caught their attention reluctantly. Both of them looked toward the doorway to his bedroom.

Gypsy stood there, lashing her tail irritably as she stared at them with baleful yellow eyes.

"I think we disturbed her," Kendall murmured.

"I wouldn't doubt it," Hawke agreed hoarsely.

With offended dignity Gypsy stalked to the door connecting the suites. Opening it with her usual deftness, she went into Kendall's suite, tail still twitching.

Bemused, Hawke and Kendall watched as a black-spotted paw reached carefully underneath the door, gripped it securely, and then drew it closed with a soft click.

"Tactful soul, isn't she," Hawke observed.

Kendall tore her eyes away from the closed door and stared at Hawke. "She's never done that before. Closed the door behind her, I mean. I wonder when she learned to do that."

"I don't know, but she's obviously on my side now."

"What do you mean *now*? She defected to your side a long time ago! Ever since you seduced her with fish."

"Speaking of seducing . . ."

"Listen to the man!"

He laughed, then sobered abruptly. "When will you marry me?" he asked softly.

"Whenever you like." Kendall laughed suddenly. "Won't Daddy be surprised!"

Hawke smiled sheepishly. "Well, as a matter of fact, he won't be."

"What?" She blinked at him. "But I haven't talked to him since I arrived here."

"I have. I've been trying to get in touch with him for days. Finally reached him through the American embassy. That was yesterday afternoon."

"But why?"

"To declare my honorable intentions, of course." Hawke grinned. "I told him that if he didn't want to miss his daughter's wedding, he'd better get here by the end of the week."

"Sure of yourself, weren't you?"

"You know better than that. By the end of the week, though, I would have been desperate enough to marry you whether you liked it or not."

"Charming." She frowned slightly. "Wait a minute, now. Are you telling me that you went through the American embassy to locate my father in South America just to tell him that you were going to marry his daughter?" When Hawke nodded, she asked uncertainly, "Have you ever met my father?"

"Not to my knowledge."

"Well, what did Daddy say?"

"He laughed a lot and said he was on his way." Ruefully, Hawke added, "He didn't seem at all surprised."

"And he told me to beware of the hawk," Kendall muttered. She stared at her Hawke wryly. "Has your mother, by any chance, been trying to marry you off?"

"Constantly. Do you smell a conspiracy?"

"Don't you?" She sighed. "Ten to one we find out at the wedding that they know each other."

Hawke chuckled. "Then we'll have to thank them, won't we?"

Pushing the speculation from her mind, Kendall smiled invitingly. "Speaking of thanking . . ."

"Yes?" he asked.

"When are you going to thank me—properly—for your medallion? I think my feelings are hurt!"

"I'm going to *start* thanking you right now," he replied somewhat hoarsely, lifting her into his arms with the easy strength that always had the power to steal her breath. Striding toward the bedroom, he added, "And it may take a while."

Reaching the bed, he tossed her playfully onto the middle of it, and Kendall bounced a couple of times, laughing. "You forgot to make sure we won't be interrupted," she pointed out happily.

"You're so right." Hawke bent over to take the phone off the hook, then turned and went into the sitting room. Kendall heard the door open and shut, and the distinct sound of the bolt being thrown. Then he was back with her.

Almost as if it were the first time for them, they undressed each other lovingly. Playful at first, but not for long.

Passion flared between them, and the playful caresses became fierce, hungry. They couldn't get enough of one another, holding, touching, kissing.

Hawke raked his fingers through her hair, staring down at her with that intensity she no longer feared, that expression she now recognized as a love greater than she had believed possible. A love matched by her own for him.

"I'll build you a castle," he vowed huskily. "I'll surround you with beauty and love and laughter—take care of you. And if I can't scare away the nightmares, then I'll be there to hold you until they don't matter."

"Not a castle," she murmured, tracing his lips with trembling fingers. "Just a home. I haven't had a home in a very long time. I want to live with you here on your island and build a family."

His eyes flared with that fierce, loving possession. "A large family. Lots of little silver-haired girls with their mother's eyes."

"And dark-haired boys with sinful charm!" Kendall wrapped her arms tightly around his neck. "Love me, Hawke . . . I need you so much. . . ."

"And I need you. . . ." His hands moved over her body

with hungry eagerness, rediscovering all the secret areas of pleasure. Touching her as though the feel of her smooth golden flesh was an addiction he had developed.

Kendall moaned as she felt his mouth on first one nipple and then the other, felt his hands shaping her willing body. Her own hands were far from still, moving over his muscled form. She could hardly bear to stop touching him.

And then the passion exploded between them, beyond their control, and they joined in a violent, exhilarating consummation. It took them to an enchanted land, a woman wearing a glittering golden hawk and a man wearing a gleaming opal unicorn, and left them at last to drift slowly home.

It was a long time before Kendall could summon the strength for speech, and when she did speak, it was in a wry voice. "There's something vaguely indecent about this, you know. Making love in broad daylight."

"The hell you say." Hawke sounded amused.

"I didn't say that I didn't like it. Please don't misunderstand." Kendall rested an elbow on his chest and stared down at him gravely. "In fact, I think it could become a habit. Aren't you shocked?"

"Terribly. I've caught myself an utterly shameless woman. Thank God." He opened his eyes finally and stared up at her. "Which reminds me . . . for someone who was amazingly innocent this time yesterday, you catch on very quickly."

"Thank you. I had a very good teacher." She lifted a rueful

eyebrow. "You'll notice that I'm not asking you where you learned to be such an experienced lover."

"It's a gift, actually."

"From the gods, no doubt."

"Precisely."

"Modest, aren't you?"

Hawke chuckled softly. "You'll have to reform me. In fact, we'll make it a mutual effort. I'll reform you too."

"Why? I'm perfect."

"You get yourself into too much trouble. Jumping out of planes and getting locked in with harems. And learning how to play poker in jail."

"That was before," she declared, biting back a giggle. "If it hadn't been for your little schemes, I would have been a pattern of respectability here."

"Nevertheless, I don't intend to spend half my time wondering what you're up to. I don't see how your father stood it for fifteen years. The man has courage."

"Don't forget a sense of humor."

"That too."

Kendall propped her chin on her hand. "You're still sore because I beat you at poker."

"Pride suffered a blow, I'll admit, but it recovered when I beat you at chess. And tennis."

"Don't forget sailboarding."

"An oversight."

She tugged at the hair on his chest with a little more force than necessary. "You're being modest again."

"Ouch. Sorry."

"So tell me." Kendall smiled innocently. "How do you plan to keep me out of trouble? You can't just lock me up in the suite or chain me to your bed."

"Why not?"

"People would wonder. Besides, I know how to pick locks."

Hawke lifted both eyebrows, staring at her with a laugh in his eyes. "Oh, really? There must be a good story in that."

Casually, she told him, "I learned from a strange little man in Europe. He swore he was the best thief in the world. I didn't believe him though. He kept getting caught."

"My God," Hawke laughed faintly, then added in a stronger tone, "You see? I wouldn't have a moment's peace!"

"What are you going to do about it?" she teased.

"Easy. I'll just keep you barefoot and pregnant, and you won't have time to get into trouble."

"*Hawke!*" Her laughter faded suddenly, and she gazed into his eyes with a tender smile. "That's a reform I'd enjoy very much."

"Good." He shaped her face with gentle hands. "Because I know a good thing when I find one, honey. You're stuck with me—for the rest of our lives."

"I'll go along with that," she breathed huskily, just before his lips touched hers.

Four months of marriage to Hawke had given Kendall a peace she had never known before—and a glow that caused all the hotel guests to smile at her bemusedly. She and Hawke were obviously ecstatically happy.

Kendall stepped off the elevator early one morning, wearing a pair of indecently short shorts and a halter top that Hawke had taken instant exception to. Her good news, however, had smoothed the frown from his brow. It had also sent them back to bed for an extended period of nonverbal communication.

She had left Hawke shaving and humming fatuous songs to himself and Gypsy, while she slipped downstairs. She had to find Rick. There was one last question . . . and it was driving her *bananas!*

She cornered the hotel manager by the unoccupied desk, and pinned him with a look he had already learned implied the steel beneath her innocent exterior. "Rick. *Where* did he get the scar?"

Rick shifted uneasily and gave her a pleading look. "Kendall, it's been nearly fifteen years, and I swore—"

Kendall assumed a wounded expression and folded her

hands over her tanned, still-flat stomach. "It's not good for things to prey on an expectant mother's mind," she announced, aggrieved. "You wouldn't want anything to happen your unborn godchild, would you?"

Rick stared at her for a moment, his startled gaze dropping unconsciously to her stomach. Then a cockeyed grin tugged at the corners of his mouth. "Really? You and Hawke are—"

"Yes," she cut him off ruthlessly, "we are. And if you don't want me to be a basket case for the next seven months, you'll tell me where Hawke got that scar!"

His grin remained. "Well . . . I know you'll tell Hawke, but I just can't stand it anymore! It's like this. We all got drunk one night, and decided to take Hawke to a tattoo parlor and . . ."

Hawke emerged from the elevator sometime later to the sounds of sheer unbridled mirth. The source of the disturbance seemed to be the desk, and half the guests in the building were standing around it with uncertain grins and puzzled eyes.

The lobby was the place to be, after all.

Several long strides took Hawke through the crowd and to the desk, where he discovered his erring wife and erstwhile best friend, both doubled over with laughter. He didn't really have to ask, but he did anyway. Staring at the former friend, who was trying to wipe tears from his eyes, he said carefully, "You told her, didn't you?"

Before Rick could answer, Kendall pulled herself upright by clutching the edge of the desk and stared at him in horrified amusement. "Hawke—that scar! Darling, you didn't . . . you *couldn't* have! No wonder you can't remember! It's the funniest thing—" Her voice became choked with laughter.

Unsure whether or not the crowd around them had heard the whole story, Hawke nonetheless felt a tide of red creeping up his lean cheeks. Hastily, he gathered up his laughing wife, striding toward the elevator and telling her fiercely, *"You* are going to tell me where that damned scar came from!"

"Oh, no!" Kendall was laughing almost too hard to speak. "I—I'll have something to hold over your head whenever you get too domineering!"

"Kendall, you *will* tell me!" he ordered in his most commanding voice, shifting her slight weight so that he could press the button to summon the elevator.

"No way!"

By the time the elevator doors slid open, Hawke's commanding tone had altered to a pleading one. "Honey, for God's sake—I have to know! *What happened that night?"*

Kendall only laughed harder, clutching his neck and hiding her face against his throat.

As the elevator doors began to close behind the hotel's

favorite couple, the fascinated crowd in the lobby heard a few words more—and nothing to satisfy their rampant curiosity.

"Hell. I'll never live this down. Maybe plastic surgery . . . ?"

"Oh, God—the doctor's *face!*"

About the Author

KAY HOOPER is indisputably one of the top romance writers today. Known for the wit and sensuality of her writing, Kay is beloved by readers and critics alike and has over four million copies of her romances in print. She lives in North Carolina.